The sexual tension **them had been palpable downstairs in the restaurant earlier, and it was even deeper now that they had actually talked and then danced together.**

"Have dinner with me tomorrow night," Darius prompted abruptly as he turned to place a restraining hand on her arm before they could reach the table where her sister and brother-in-law were waiting for her.

"I— What— No!" Miranda looked totally flustered by the invitation.

"Why on earth not?" He scowled darkly.

She gave an impatient shake of her head. "As I said, I'm grateful to you for inviting us up to your club, and—and everything else. It's made my birthday even more special. I just— This— You and me— It isn't going anywhere."

"I only invited you out to dinner, Miranda, not to become the mother of my children," he pointed out drily.

The color deepened in her cheeks. "And when was the last time you invited a woman out to dinner without the expectation of taking her to bed at the end of the evening?" Her pointed chin rose challengingly as she looked up at him.

"And what makes you so sure that isn't going to happen?" he purred.

Andy wasn't sure of anything in regard to her undeniable and unexpected attraction to this man; that was the problem!

The Twin Tycoons

Twin billionaire brothers—one dark and brooding, one blond and charming. Who would you choose?

Billionaire brothers Darius and Xander Sterne have it all—power, wealth and the world at their beck and call. Never challenged, always triumphant—*nothing* is unattainable when you own the world, and they've enjoyed every indulgence their affluent status affords them.

Until now.

Because these twin tycoons are about to learn there are some things money and power can't buy... And that the greatest challenges net the most satisfying rewards.

Find out what happens in:

The Redemption of Darius Sterne
February 2015

The Taming of Xander Sterne
March 2015

Carole Mortimer

The Redemption of Darius Sterne

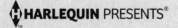

HARLEQUIN PRESENTS®

Recycling programs
for this product may
not exist in your area.

ISBN-13: 978-0-373-13789-3

The Redemption of Darius Sterne

First North American Publication 2015

Printed in U.S.A.

Carole Mortimer was born in and lives in the UK. She is married to Peter and they have six sons. She has been writing for Harlequin since 1978 and has written almost 200 books. She writes for the Harlequin Presents and Harlequin Historical lines. Carole is a *USA TODAY* bestselling author, and in 2012 she was recognized by Queen Elizabeth II for her "outstanding contribution to literature."

Other titles by Carole Mortimer available in ebook:

For Peter, as always.

CHAPTER ONE

'WHO IS *THAT*?' Andy exclaimed as she glanced towards the doorway of the exclusive restaurant and bar, Midas, in which she was currently celebrating with her sister and brother-in-law.

Her glass of champagne raised halfway to her lips, Andy openly stared across the elegant restaurant at the man standing just inside the doorway. Tall and grimly unsmiling, he removed his dark outer coat, before handing it off to the waiting *maître d'*.

Andy estimated him to be in his early to mid-thirties, and he was so dark and arrestingly handsome that Andy couldn't have looked away if her life had depended on it.

Everything about the man was dark, she noted as she continued to watch him.

The elegant black suit and the shirt and tie he wore under it, the perfect tailoring emphasising rather than hiding the muscled perfection of his well over six feet height.

His tousled hair gleamed the colour of dark mahogany under the light of the overhead crystal chandeliers.

His complexion was olive.

As for his *expression*...

The longer she stared at him, the more Andy realised that grim didn't even begin to describe the look on that hard and chiselled face. He had a high, intelligent forehead, glowering dark brows over narrowed eyes, blades for cheekbones, a sculptured and firmly unsmiling mouth, his jaw square and arrogant.

Overall the combined effect was best described as electrifying.

There really was no other word that quite described the man as he now glanced disinterestedly about the elegant restaurant, while at the same time continuing his conversation with the man accompanying him. A piercing glance, which now moved over and past Andy, and then slowly moved back again, before stopping.

Andy's breath caught in her throat, her mind going completely blank as she found herself the focus of that piercing gaze.

For some reason Andy had expected that the man's eyes would be as darkly arresting as the rest of him, but instead they were a clear and beautiful topaz in colour, with darker striations fanning out from the pitch-black pupils.

They were mesmerising eyes, which continued to hold Andy's gaze captive even as he raised one questioningly dark brow at her obvious interest.

'Aha!' her sister murmured beside her as she saw the direction of Andy's gaze and realised the reason for her earlier comment. 'Absolutely gorgeous, isn't he?'

'Sorry?' Andy was still held captive by that compelling gaze as she answered Kim distractedly, her heart pounding in her chest, her pulse racing.

'The man you're currently ogling, darling,' her sister teased dryly. 'Don't you just want to rip his clothes off and—?'

'Hello? Husband sitting right next to you,' Colin reminded Kim ruefully.

'That doesn't stop me from window-shopping, my love,' his wife replied pertly.

'There's window-shopping, and then there's just completely out of your price range!' Colin muttered teasingly.

'That's the whole point of window-shopping, silly!' Kim chuckled affectionately.

Andy was barely aware of the bantering between her sister and brother-in-law, the stranger's gaze continuing to hold hers captive for several more, heart-stoppingly long seconds, before he gave a curl of his top lip in the semblance of a smile. Then he turned away, as he and his dining companion now followed the *maître d'* to their table.

Andy drew in a ragged breath, although her heart was still pounding, her pulse racing.

A small shiver waved over her body, a reminder of her unexpected physical reaction to that darkly delicious man.

And she was far from the only one watching the two men as they made their way through the restaurant, nodding acknowledgement to several acquaintances as they passed, before stopping at a table for four near the window. They greeted an older couple already seated there, before the *maître d'* himself pulled back the two empty chairs so that the two men could join them.

In fact, now that Andy was no longer completely under his spell she realised that the other diners weren't just surreptitiously watching those two men, but that conversation in the room had become a hushed whisper; the very air seemed to be filled with tense expectation.

Which, considering this fashionable restaurant, was frequented only by the rich and the famous, who were usually too full of their own self-importance to be aware of anyone else's, she found distinctly intriguing.

In fact, Andy had been slightly overwhelmed by the clientele when she'd first arrived.

The only reason that Andy and her sister and brother-in-law were able to dine in such exalted company at all was because Colin worked in the London office of Midas Enterprises. As an employee of Midas he was allowed to book a table at one of the Midas restaurants for himself and three guests once a year, and given an employee discount; none of them would ever have been able to afford to eat here otherwise!

The same didn't apply to the Midas nightclub on the floor above; that was reserved for members only. And to become a member, you had to be approved by both the Sterne brothers, the billionaire owners of Midas Enterprises.

As well as most of the known universe, it seemed to Andy.

Social hermit that she usually was, even she had heard of Darius and Xander Sterne's success. Her brother-in-law had told her that the brothers had burst onto the business scene twelve years ago, when they had launched an Internet social media company, which had rapidly grown and grown, until they'd sold it just three years later for several billion pounds. After that there had been no stopping them, as they'd bought up several electronic companies, an airline, media and film-production companies, hotel chains, and opened up exclusive restaurants and clubs just like this one, all around the world.

Everything they touched, it seemed, did turn to gold.

Which was probably the reason they had decided to name their company Midas.

'Don't let it worry you, Andy.' Her sister now gave her hand a reassuring pat as she saw that grimace. 'Everyone, male or female, reacts in exactly the same way the first time they set eyes on the Sterne brothers.'

'The Sterne brothers?' Andy repeated breathlessly, eyes wide; no wonder everyone in the restaurant was staring!

'The Sterne twins, to be exact,' Kim corrected knowledgeably.

'Twins?' Andy's eyes widened incredulously. 'Are you saying that there's another one just like him at home?' There couldn't possibly be!

The man who had just walked into the restaurant was—well, he was utterly unique. In a dark and compelling way Andy could never imagine anyone else ever being. Certainly not in the form of an identical twin.

She knew little of the Sterne brothers' personal lives. When they had first rocketed into the public eye she had only been thirteen and at ballet school, and totally caught up in that world. She had paid little attention to the world of business, or society photographs in newspapers and glossy magazines of the rich and the famous.

And after her accident she had been too busy trying to rebuild her future to be too aware of what was going on in other people's lives.

She had known her brother-in-law had worked for Midas Enterprises for the last few years, of course, but the bachelor billionaire Sterne brothers inhabited a totally different world from her own—no doubt they could eat at a different one of their own restaurants every night around the world, and fly there on their own private jet!

But she would certainly have remembered it if she had ever seen so much as a photograph of the man seated across the restaurant.

'Hardly, darling. That's his twin sitting beside him,' Kim explained softly.

Andy's gaze shifted to the man who had walked in with Mr Dark and Compelling—Darius or Xander Sterne?—and now sat at the table with him talking to the older couple.

Definitely not an identical twin!

If one of the twins was dark and compelling then the other was light and magnetic; the second man's fashionably tousled hair was a pale blond, his skin golden, a sexy grin lighting up his handsome and chiselled features, laughter lines fanning out from warm brown eyes, as if he smiled often. He was as tall and muscled as his brother, his impeccably black evening suit also tailored to perfection.

Under any other circumstances Andy knew she would have found the second twin the most handsome man in the room, but the dark twin was just so breathtaking she had to admit to having barely noticed his brother until now.

Dark twin. Light twin.

Andy's gaze moved inexorably back to the dark twin. 'Which one is he?'

'Mr Gorgeous? That would be Xander,' Kim supplied lightly.

'Hello? I'm still sitting here,' Colin put in pointedly, his own dark-haired and blue-eyed looks better described as homely rather than gorgeous.

'You know how much I love you, love,' Kim assured him warmly. 'But no woman in her right mind could stop herself from looking at someone like Xander Sterne.'

Again, Andy was barely listening to her

sister and Colin as they bantered back and forth. Mainly because the dark twin had just glanced her way again. And given another raise of that dark and mocking brow as he'd found her still watching him. Causing Andy to quickly look away, the warmth of embarrassed colour flooding her cheeks.

'—all that gorgeous golden hair and those warm brown eyes. As for the delicious and toned body underneath that wonderful designer-label suit...' Kim continued to sing the man's praises.

'I'm going to go to the bathroom, leaving you two ladies to continue drooling, before I develop a complex,' Colin excused dryly as he stood up and left the table.

'Xander is the blond one?' Andy questioned her sister sharply once the two of them were alone, instantly revising her thoughts as she realised it was *Darius* she had been staring at, not the light twin, Xander.

'Well, of course he's the gorgeous blond,' Kim teased dismissively. 'I would hardly be drooling, as Colin so elegantly put it, over Darius.' She gave a shiver. 'All that dark, cold broodiness makes him just too scary for words!'

Dark, cold and scary.

Yes, Andy acknowledged, Darius Sterne was definitely scary. But, as far as she was concerned, not in the cold and brooding way her sister meant.

If Xander was light and good humour, then Darius was the opposite; a man as dark as sin —inside as well as out. His chiselled features were so grimly forbidding it looked as if he rarely found occasion to smile, let alone laugh.

But when he did?

How would it feel to be the woman responsible for putting a smile on that coldly arrogant face? To bathe in his appreciative laughter? To be the one responsible for putting the warmth of that laughter into those beautiful topaz eyes?

Or the heat of desire!

And on that note Andy brought her thoughts to a screeching halt.

Men like Darius Sterne, successful *billionaires* like Darius Sterne, she corrected herself ruefully, did not look at women like her. Women who so obviously did not even belong in a restaurant like Midas, let alone the rarefied world of extreme wealth that the Sterne brothers inhabited.

And yet Darius Sterne had certainly looked at her.

Only briefly, Andy admitted, but he had definitely returned her gaze.

Maybe that was because she had been caught staring at him eyes wide, mouth agape?

Well, yes. Maybe. But to be fair, everyone else in the restaurant had also been staring at the Sterne twins. Maybe not in quite the lustful way she had been staring at Darius Sterne, but they *had* all been looking, nonetheless.

Lustful?

Lord, yes, her feelings were lustful, if the tingling fullness in her breasts and the heat surging through her body was any indication!

And Andy was sure it was.

Though she had never, ever, responded in such a visceral way to any man before tonight. Before she'd looked at Darius Sterne and been unable to look away again.

Until the age of nineteen, her life and her emotions had all been totally dedicated to ballet and her career, with no time left for romance. After the months of recovering from the accident, Andy had had necessarily to concentrate on making something else of her life.

Her dream of one day becoming a world-class ballerina had been over, but she was by no means a quitter, and had no intentions of just sitting around feeling sorry for herself. Consequently she had known she had to *do* something with her life.

It had been a lot of hard work, and taken most of her own share of the money left to her and Kim by their parents when they'd died almost five years ago. But three years after making that decision, Andy had finished her training to teach and been able to open a ballet studio for five-to-sixteen-year-olds. Ballet was what she knew, after all. And maybe one day, if she was lucky, she might actually be responsible for discovering and training a world-class ballerina.

Her personal life had been the casualty of all those years of hard work, both as a ballerina and latterly her training to teach others to dance. As a consequence she'd had no intimate relationships before her accident. Or since…

The loss of both her beloved parents had been a terrible blow, and Andy had buried herself even more in her love of ballet as a way of coping with that loss. The accident just months later, putting an end to her career in ballet, had shaken her to her very core.

Oh, she had recovered some of her previous confidence these past four years, on the outside at least. But the physical scars that now marred her body were undeniable. She certainly hadn't ever wanted to share those with any man.

Most especially a man as handsome and sophisticated as Darius Sterne, who no doubt dated some of the most beautiful women in the world. He certainly wouldn't be interested in someone like Andy, who was scarred emotionally on the inside, and visibly on the outside.

'Darius?'

Darius masked his irritation as he gave the beautiful blonde across the restaurant one last appreciative glance before turning his attention slowly back to the three people seated at the table with him. His twin Xander. His mother. And stepfather.

Darius had managed to block them all out in his preoccupation with the fragile-looking woman, having quickly assessed her dining companions when he arrived, and just as quickly dismissed them; the likeness between the two women, in colouring and facial features, meant they were probably sisters, and the man's close proximity to the second woman showed he was with her rather than the woman who held Darius's interest. There was no fourth place setting at the table, either.

The woman was ethereally beautiful, her ash-blonde hair a straight curtain to just below her shoulders, green eyes huge in the delicate perfection of her face. It was those hauntingly lovely green eyes that had first caught and held his attention the moment he'd entered the restaurant.

Surprisingly.

Because she wasn't his usual type at all; his taste usually ran towards women who were older, and more sophisticated than the youthful-looking blonde. Women who expected nothing more from him than a night or two in his bed.

But there was something about the green-eyed blonde that had caught and held his attention.

Possibly because something about her seemed slightly familiar to him? The tilt of her head... The elegance of her movement...

And yet at the same time Darius knew he had never met her before; he would surely have remembered where and when if he had!

Maybe it was her other-worldly air that had caught his notice? She was so willowy she looked as if a puff of wind might blow her over, her bare arms incredibly slender, her collarbones and the hollows of her throat visible above the neckline of her black dress. Her face was hauntingly lovely; eyes fringed by thick dark lashes, cheekbones high, straight nose, full and sensuous lips, with a pointed, stubborn chin. That straight ash-blonde hair had the appearance of moonbeams, tempting a man to run his fingers through its silkiness.

Moonbeams?

He could never remember waxing lyrical about the colour and texture of a woman's hair before.

Whatever the reason for his attraction to her, Darius had the definite feeling it was reciprocated, as he had felt those beautiful green eyes continuing to watch him through the curtain of her thick dark lashes as he and Xander strolled through the restaurant to join his mother and stepfather at their table.

But maybe a more plausible reason for having become so preoccupied by the blonde was that he didn't really want to be here at the restaurant at all?

It was Darius's reluctance to start the evening that had caused him to work so late at his office he hadn't even had time to go to his apartment and change before meeting up with Xander outside the restaurant. The two of them had decided during a telephone call earlier today that presenting a united front tonight was probably the best policy.

His mother's frown of disapproval, when

he had bent to place the perfunctory kiss on her smooth and powdered cheek, had clearly told him that she had taken note that Xander and their stepfather were both wearing black evening clothes and Darius wasn't.

Not that it had bothered Darius for many years whether or not he had his mother's approval. Twenty years, to be exact. Since the death of the father he and Xander had hated and the husband Catherine had feared. The man that Darius so resembled, in looks, at least; no doubt it was difficult for Catherine to even look at the son who so reminded her of the husband she had disliked.

Darius could understand some of his mother's aversion but it didn't stop her rejection from hurting him. Over the years he had found the best way to deal with that hurt was to distance himself from his mother in return. It was not the ideal, by any means, but as the years had passed it had become the best way for him to deal with the situation.

Consequently mother and son now rarely talked, let alone spent evenings together like this.

Thankfully the rest of his family usually more than made up for Darius's brooding silences.

Xander was currently behaving with his usual charming urbanity.

Their mother, Catherine, still beautiful at fifty-eight, was also presenting a gracious and charming front for the benefit of the other diners, who they were all only too well aware were continuing to watch the family surreptitiously.

Only Charlie, or Charles, as his mother preferred her second husband to be called, was being his usual warm and affable self as he ignored the other diners, and the underlying tensions at their table, in favour of keeping the conversation light and impersonal.

It might be Catherine's birthday today, and the reason they were all sitting here, but his relationship with his mother was now such that it was out of respect and affection for Charlie that Darius had made the effort to make an appearance at all this evening.

'Isn't it time we drank the toast to your birthday, Mother?' He picked up his glass of champagne. 'I can't stay long. I have somewhere else I need to be.' He glanced towards the back of the restaurant where the second blonde's escort had disappeared a few minutes ago. Probably on his way to the men's room.

His mother gave another frown of disapproval. 'Surely you can spare me one evening of your time, Darius?'

'Unfortunately not,' he cut her off unapologetically.

'You speak to him, Charles!' Catherine turned to appeal to her husband.

'You heard the boy, Catherine, he has work he needs to do.'

Silver-haired, and in his mid-sixties, Charles Latimer obviously adored his wife, and Darius knew that the older man did everything in his power to ensure her happiness. But even Charlie knew better than to argue when Darius made a statement in that flat, uncompromising tone.

'He didn't say it was work.'

'It is,' Darius bit out tersely, deliberately choosing to ignore Xander's accusing glare.

He had turned up tonight, hadn't he? Had made the required appearance at his mother's private birthday dinner celebrations, as he would make an appearance at the more public celebrations next weekend, at a dinner given in aid of one of his mother's numerous charities. What more did any of them want from him? Whatever it was, the estrangement between Darius and his mother was now such that he wasn't willing to give it.

He gave another glance towards the back of the restaurant, having just decided exactly what he *did* want.

* * *

'It *was* Xander you were looking at, wasn't it?' Kim questioned with concern. Three years older than Andy, she had always taken her 'protective big sister' role very seriously, even more so since the loss of their parents.

Andy didn't reply immediately, continuing to watch Darius Sterne as he suddenly stood up abruptly from his table.

The woman seated at the table with the three men was beautiful, but obviously aged in her fifties, and with her blonde hair and dark eyes she bore a resemblance to Xander Sterne. Perhaps she was the twins' mother? Although Andy could see no resemblance to Darius whatsoever.

The older man didn't look like either of the brothers, so perhaps he was the twins' step-father?

Whatever the relationship between the Sterne twins and the older couple, it had been impossible not to miss the edge of tension at the table since the twins sat down. A tension that seemed to ease as Darius Sterne now left their company.

Andy's gaze continued to follow him as he walked towards the back of the restaurant.

'No,' she finally answered her sister distractedly, her breath leaving her in a whoosh as Darius disappeared from view down a marble corridor at the back of the restaurant.

Allowing her to realise she had actually stopped breathing, as well as being unable to take her eyes off him until he disappeared, his elegance of movement so like that of a stalking predator. A sleek and powerful jaguar, perhaps, or maybe a tiger? Definitely something feral and lethal!

'I advise you not to even bother looking at Darius Sterne, Andy,' Kim said hastily. 'Admittedly he's gorgeous, in a dark and dangerously compelling way, but he's also way out of your league, my love. Well out of any sane woman's league!' her sister added with feeling.

Andy took a much-needed sip of the champagne in her glass; her mouth had gone dry just from watching Darius Sterne.

'There have been stories and hints in the newspapers for years regarding the extent of Darius Sterne's darkness,' Kim cautioned as Andy made no reply.

She turned to give her sister a teasing smile. 'You aren't saying he's into black magic?'

'More like wielding whips and paddles.'

Andy almost choked on her champagne. 'Kim!' she finally managed to splutter incredulously. 'Why is everyone so obsessed with that stuff nowadays?' Personally, she could imagine nothing more demeaning to a woman than having some man put his collar of ownership on her and demanding she call him master. Or tying her to his bed before doing whatever he wanted with her. Or that same man demanding that she kneel subserviently at his feet until he told her otherwise. It made Andy's skin crawl just to think about any man treating a woman like that.

Even a man she found as fascinating as Darius Sterne.

Her sister held up her hands defensively. 'I'm not responsible for the gossip about him.'

'You're responsible for reading it,' Andy scolded. 'What's printed in the gutter press isn't gossip, Kim, it's pure fantasy most of the time. Sensationalised speculation, and luridly made-up headlines to encourage people to buy their newspaper rather than someone else's.'

Her sister shrugged slender shoulders. 'You've heard the saying, there's no smoke without fire.'

She raised her brows. 'I also remember Mum telling us years ago that it isn't wise, or fair, to listen to gossip or hearsay, that we should make our own minds up about other people.'

'*If* Mum were here, I have no doubts she

would also tell you that there's nothing in the least wise in being attracted to a man like Darius Sterne,' her sister stated with certainty.

Both girls sobered at the mention of their mother. At the time of their parents' deaths the sisters, Kim twenty-one, and Andy eighteen, had been absolutely devastated by the loss, but with the passing of time they had both come to appreciate the years they had been able to spend with their parents. Andy had always been grateful that at least they had lived long enough to see Kim happily married to Colin, and they had also been present the night Andy had appeared in the lead of *Giselle* with England's most reputable ballet company.

Andy's own accident, just six months after their death, had meant that she would never dance in public again.

Andy determinedly shook off the sadness that realisation still gave her, even four years later. She had her studio, was slowly, sometimes too slowly, making a success of it. She also conveniently lived in the flat above the studio. It was so much more than a lot of people had.

'I really wouldn't worry about it, Kim; I'm never likely to so much as set eyes on Darius Sterne again, so it really isn't an issue,' she pointed out ruefully. 'As you said, it's nice to window-shop.'

'You ladies are never going to believe what just happened to me in the Gents,' a red-faced Colin announced as he arrived back at their table before plonking himself back down into his seat to look at them both expectantly.

His wife raised her eyebrows. 'Do we want to know?'

'Oh, yes.' He nodded with certainty. 'It was nothing like that, Kim!' He frowned at his wife as her eyebrows had risen even higher. 'Honestly, sometimes I wonder if your mind isn't constantly in the gutter.'

'I think we just had this conversation.' Andy chuckled as she gave her sister a pointed glance. 'Kim's just been regaling me with lurid tales of the licentious behaviour of the Sterne twins,' she explained at Colin's questioning glance.

'*One* of the Sterne twins,' Kim defended. 'I'm sure that Xander is every bit as deliciously gentlemanly and uncomplicated as he appears to be.'

Andy gave a disbelieving snort; Xander Sterne might not be as obviously brooding as his twin brother, but there was no way a man of his age and wealth, and with those Adonis good looks, could possibly have remained single if he was as gentlemanly and uncomplicated as Kim claimed he was.

Admittedly, with that much money, the Sterne brothers could no doubt pick and choose when it came to women. As it would no doubt be difficult for either of the brothers to ever know if a woman wanted them for themselves, or their billions. But even so, it was unusual for two brothers, aged in their early to mid-thirties, never to have married.

Or at least Andy assumed neither of them had ever married; she really knew very little about them. They could both be married for all she knew, but had left their wives and half a dozen children at home this evening.

If that was true, it made Darius Sterne's earlier flirtation with her decidedly questionable.

Andy decided there and then to look the Sterne brothers up on the Internet as soon as she got home. With special emphasis on learning a lot more about Darius.

'Do I take it from that remark that it's Darius Sterne you've been gossiping about?' Colin gave Kim an irritated glance. 'You do realise that he's one of my employers? That we wouldn't even be here this evening if he wasn't? Talk about biting—literally—the hand that feeds you!' he added crossly.

Kim's cheeks coloured guiltily. 'I was only repeating what I've read in the newspapers and magazines.'

'Those glossy magazines you read that rave about a couple's marital bliss one month, and then unashamedly write about their break-up the next?' her husband came back scathingly.

'He has you there, Kim.' Andy smiled.

Her sister adopted a look of hurt superiority. 'You were going to tell us what just happened to you in the men's room, Colin?'

'Oh. Yes.' His youthfully handsome face lit up excitedly again as he sat forward. 'Anyway, I was just drying my hands, when who do you think walked in the door?'

Andy's heart suddenly skipped a beat, her breath once again ceasing in her lungs, as she suddenly knew *exactly* who had entered the men's room.

The same person who, just minutes after Colin, had also disappeared down that marble hallway in the direction of the loo.

'Darius Sterne,' Colin confirmed excitedly. 'Not only that but he actually spoke to me. I've worked for the brothers for seven years now, seen them around the building of course, but I've never spoken to either one of them before tonight.'

Kim gave Andy a narrow-eyed glance before turning back to her husband. 'What did he say?'

'You're never going to believe it!' her husband assured her. 'I can hardly believe it myself.'

'What did he say, Colin?' Kim bit out through gritted teeth.

'Well, if you stopped interrupting me maybe I'd have chance to tell you,' he teased, obviously enjoying himself now that he had their full attention.

'Andy, you can bear witness to just how annoying my husband is being right now—because I am seriously going to strangle him if he doesn't tell us what Darius said to him, in the next thirty seconds.' Kim's hazel-coloured eyes sparkled warningly.

Andy was too transfixed by Colin's air of excitement to take her sister's threat in the least seriously. Especially when she was sure that Kim had to be just as eager as she was to hear what Darius had said to Colin to make him look so excited.

CHAPTER TWO

DARIUS'S EXPRESSION WAS grim as he looked down into the Midas nightclub from the window in his executive office on the second floor.

The club was busy tonight, as it was every night, the glamorous and the famous all wishing to see or be seen as patrons of the fashionable and prestigious members-only Midas nightclub.

Everything about the club spoke of the same opulence as the restaurant on the ground floor; the walls up here were covered in gold silk paper, the dance floor the same gleaming black marble as the pillars supporting the second-floor gallery, where people could stand and talk or just observe the other patrons. The tables placed about the club were rounds of black marble, on gold pedestals, surrounded by comfortable black leather armchairs and sofas.

And Darius, hands in the pockets of his

trousers, was able to stand and observe it all, from his aerie on the second floor.

The coloured lights swept across the dance floor full of bodies gyrating to the heavy beat of the loud music. The quietly efficient bar staff, dressed in their black uniforms, were serving champagne and cocktails and everything in between to the people standing about the bar, or sitting at the tables that edged the dance floor. There were curved, leather-seated booths further back in the nightclub, for those patrons wishing for a more private, intimate evening.

It was to one of those booths in particular that Darius's gaze had kept drifting for the past half an hour as he stood at the window looking out.

It was a booth that continued to remain empty, despite the reserved sign sitting in the centre of the black marble tabletop.

Darius's mouth tightened in irritation with his own feelings of disappointment. Despite her youth, and the delicacy of appearance, he had hoped that the green-eyed blonde would accept the challenge he had laid down by inviting her and her family up to the nightclub as his guests. That the interest he had seen in her eyes would at least make her curious enough to encourage her family to accept that invitation. Learning during his conversation with Colin Freeman that the other man actually worked for one of Darius's companies had been something of a bonus, after he had all but stalked the man into the Gents.

Even so, the emptiness of that reserved booth now continued to mock him.

He had been a fool to expect anything else. So the beautiful blonde hadn't been able to take her eyes off him earlier. So what? Wasn't the mouse just as mesmerised by the cobra?

No doubt the reason for her interest earlier had been because she'd known exactly who he was, and she had heard those dark rumours about Darius Sterne and been fascinated by the danger he represented. A danger that was no doubt the complete opposite of her own safe little life. An arm's-length danger that she felt comfortable viewing across a crowded restaurant, but didn't have the courage to actually meet head-on. As she didn't have the courage to meet Darius face to—

There was the merest prickling sensation of warning at Darius's nape, a quiver of awareness down the length of his spine before he looked up and saw the green-eyed blonde standing at the entrance to the nightclub.

Her brother-in-law had referred to her as Andy when the two men had spoken earlier. It seemed far too masculine a name for a woman who looked so totally feminine.

Darius's narrowed gaze remained fixed on her as her brother-in-law spoke briefly to Stephen, the security man Darius had warned to expect them, before the three of them then followed the security guard into the darkness of the club.

Andy walked ahead of her sister and brother-in-law, her head held high, almost in challenge. Almost as if she knew someone was watching her. As she walked her ash-blonde hair moved silkily about her shoulders.

She was taller than Darius had thought when she was sitting down in the restaurant, possibly five-eight in her stockinged feet, putting her height at about five-ten in the two-inch-heeled black strappy sandals she wore. They were conservative heels, considering that some of the women in the club tonight were wearing heels as high as six or seven inches.

Her black dress was also modest in style; it was sleeveless, yes, revealing those bare and gracefully slender arms, but the curved neckline wasn't even low enough to reveal the soft swell of the tops of her breasts, and its knee-length was a complete contrast to the bottom-skimming dresses being worn by every other woman in the club.

Darius realised she was even less his usual type than he had initially thought she was.

'Andy is a man's name.'

Andy's fingers tightened about the stem of her champagne glass at the first sound of that huskily censorious voice coming from just behind her. A sexily throaty voice that she knew instinctively, without even needing to turn and look, belonged to none other than Darius Sterne.

After all, who else could it be?

She was pretty sure she didn't know anyone else in this place apart from Kim and Colin, who were currently out on the dance floor somewhere. And no doubt the couple were still arguing over the fact that Kim hadn't wanted to come up to the Midas nightclub at all and Colin had insisted that they had to, that it would be extremely rude of him not to take up his employer's generous invitation.

It was an argument Andy had stayed out of, mainly because her own feelings on the subject were mixed. Part of her had wanted to go up to the club to see if Darius was there, another part of her had hoped that he wouldn't be.

His presence behind her had now answered that particular question, at least.

But Darius's sudden appearance at that private booth, so soon after Colin had persuaded Kim to go and dance with him, the two of them having now totally disappeared into the midst of the other gyrating dancers, made Andy question whether or not Colin working for Midas Enterprises had been the reason they had received special treatment, after all…

She had felt as if she were being watched when they arrived at the club. As if unseen eyes were following her progress as she'd walked to the table ahead of Colin and Kim. Although a surreptitious glance around the room had revealed mild interest from several of the men present, it was not enough to have caused that quiver of awareness down the length of her spine.

Except the feeling had persisted.

Just the thought of being watched by Darius now made Andy shift uncomfortably.

She straightened her shoulders, firmly instructing her fingers to stop their trembling as she composed her expression before she turned to look up at him. There would be no wide eyes and gaping mouth for her.

Instead her breath caught in the back of her throat as she was once again struck by the immediacy of Darius Sterne as he stood just feet behind her.

There was that zing of electricity, of course, but he also looked so very tall and sinfully dark in the dimmed lighting of this part of the room.

Andy had to force herself to meet the intensity of his gaze as she moistened the sudden dryness of her lips with the tip of her tongue, before finally answering him. 'It's short for Miranda.'

Darius nodded, liking the soft huskiness of her voice. And the name Miranda. It was so much more feminine than Andy. As Miranda herself was totally feminine.

Miranda was also a name that a man could murmur fiercely into the side of a woman's throat as he thrust into her before climaxing inside her...

He was close enough to Miranda now to be able to reach out and touch the silkiness of her hair. Her skin was pale and luminescent, a soft glow against the black of her dress, and she wore little or no make-up, perhaps mascara and a soft peach lip gloss. He could see now that her eyes weren't just emerald-green, as he had thought they were earlier, but shot through with shards of gold and blue. They were unusually beautiful eyes for an unusually beautiful woman.

A beautiful woman who had once again succeeded in arousing him at a glance. An arousal that had deepened as he'd watched the moistness of her tongue sweep across the fullness of her lips before she spoke with that sexily husky voice.

A voice he could easily imagine crying out his own name as they climaxed together.

'Mind if I join you?' he prompted as a waitress appeared and placed a fourth champagne glass on the table before quietly disappearing again.

Miranda raised blonde brows in the direction of that fourth glass. 'It would appear that you already have.'

'It would, wouldn't it?' Darius acknowledged as he made no move to sit down but instead moved to stand further inside the booth, his back to the room, at the same time as he blocked Miranda from looking at anything but him.

'Do we have you to thank for the champagne?' She held up her glass.

Darius nodded. 'It's the same champagne you were drinking with your meal earlier on this evening.'

A frown appeared between those magnificent green eyes. 'You noticed that from across the room?'

'I asked the sommelier on my way out of the restaurant,' he admitted huskily as he slid into the leather seat opposite her, his gaze continuing to hold hers as he poured himself a glass of champagne.

A blush warmed her cheeks and she was the first to look away.

'We were celebrating.'

'Oh?'

She nodded. 'It's my birthday today.'

Darius found himself scowling. What were the chances of this woman's birthday being the same day as his mother's?

'I'm twenty-three today,' Miranda supplied abruptly, as if his continued silence unnerved her.

So she was ten years younger than his own thirty-three years, Darius realised—and a lifetime in experience. Yet another reason why he should just get up and walk away from this woman.

'Would you like to dance?' he heard himself say instead, his mind, or another, more demanding, part of his anatomy, obviously having other ideas on the subject.

The soft curve of her jaw instantly tensed. 'No, thank you.'

'That was a very definite no,' Darius murmured.

'I don't dance in public.' Those green eyes now met his probing gaze unblinkingly.

Darius looked at her searchingly, noting the increased tension in her shoulders, and the way her fingers had tightened about her champagne glass until the knuckles showed white. Of course, it could be that he made her nervous just by being here, but somehow he thought there was more to it than that.

'Only in private?' he prompted softly.

'Not then, either.'

'Why not?' he demanded abruptly.

She blinked at his terseness, before just as quickly regaining her composure. 'Maybe I'm just no good at it?'

Darius couldn't believe that when everything about this woman spoke of grace and poise: the delicate arch of her throat, the way she held herself so elegantly, her fingers long and tapered, her legs slender and shapely. Even her feet and toes appeared graceful in those black strappy sandals. They were graceful and elegant toes he could all too easily imagine moving caressingly along the bare length of his thigh as he made love to her.

'Now tell me the real reason,' he bit out harshly.

Andy gave an inner start, not just at Darius's perception, but also his ability to cut out all unnecessary conversation and just go straight to the point of what he wanted to know. No doubt that stood him in good stead in business, but she found it more than a little disconcerting on a personal level.

Everything about this man was disconcerting on a personal level. The perfect fit of his suit jacket over those wide and muscled shoulders. The flatness of his abdomen beneath the black shirt. The long, long length of his legs.

Those sharply arresting features, dominated by the intensity of that probing topaz gaze as it remained fixed on her so intently.

She forced a smile to her lips. 'You appear to know my name, and have helped yourself to some of my birthday champagne,' she added dryly, 'but so far you haven't even bothered to introduce yourself.'

'Let's not play games, Miranda; we're both aware that you know exactly who I am.'

Yes, of course Andy knew who he was. She just had absolutely no idea what Darius was doing even talking to her, let alone engaging in what she felt sure was, for him, flirtation.

Just looking at that hard and chiselled face was enough to tell her that this wasn't a man who would heap flowery compliments and charm on a woman in order to seduce her. That he was far too self-contained, too sure of his own attractiveness, to ever need or want to do that.

But she did believe he was flirting with her now.

Oh, yes, every single nerve-ending in Andy's body was screaming out that awareness; her nipples were hard buds against the soft material of her dress and there was a heat, a swelling, between her thighs.

Darius Sterne was definitely flirting with her. Andy just had no idea why he was even bothering with someone like her when there were so many glamorously beautiful women in the room. Women who would be only too happy to dance or do anything else with or *for* him.

'Of course.' She nodded. 'It was very kind of you to extend an invitation to Colin and his family to come up and enjoy your nightclub, Mr Sterne.'

'I thought I said no games, Miranda,' he bit out challengingly.

She eyed him warily. 'I don't know what you mean.'

'We both know I invited *you* to come up to my nightclub, Miranda, so that the two of *us* could meet,' he corrected harshly. 'Your sister and brother-in-law were incidental to that invitation.'

Andy swept a slightly hounded glance in the direction of the dance floor, silently cursing when she still couldn't see Kim and Colin amongst the writhing bodies, let alone send one of them a silent plea for help. She was finding it more and more difficult to maintain any semblance of polite conversation with a man who just refused to reciprocate that politeness.

'You still haven't answered my question as to why it is you don't dance in public.'

Andy felt decidedly uncomfortable at being the focus of the intensity of this man. It was as if Darius could see into the very depths of her soul. And that by doing so he was also able to see all of her hopes and dreams.

And how most of them had been shattered four years ago.

That notion was ridiculous. This man didn't know the first thing about her.

'Hell, now I realise why you seemed familiar to me earlier,' he murmured slowly. 'You're the ballerina Miranda Jacobs.'

So he did know something about her.

He knew *everything* about her that truly mattered…

Andy drew her breath in sharply. 'Not any

more,' she bit out stiffly, very aware that her face had paled in shock, and that it was no longer just her hands that were trembling but all of her. 'Excuse me, I need to go to the bathroom!' She quickly gathered up her black clutch bag before moving along the leather seat, with the intention of making good her escape.

Only to find that escape circumvented as one of Darius's hands moved quickly across the table and his fingers clamped about her wrist. Not hard enough to actually hurt her, but definitely firmly enough to prevent her from escaping.

The intensity of his penetrating gaze was enough to cause her protest to die in her throat; she knew instinctively, that Darius simply wasn't a man who took orders, from anyone.

Andy blinked hastily as her vision blurred. She wouldn't cry. Not here, and certainly not in front of Darius Sterne. 'Please let go of my arm, Mr Sterne.'

'Darius.'

She gave a protesting shake of her head. 'Please, release me.'

He didn't remove his hand. Andy instead felt the soft pad of Darius's thumb move caressingly, soothingly, against the sensitive skin of her inner wrist. Increasing her physical awareness of him, despite the fact that seconds ago she had just wanted to escape from the painful memories his words had evoked.

'I was there that night four years ago, Miranda,' Darius stated evenly, able to feel the wild fluttering of her pulse beneath the pad of his thumb, to see the look of pained shock in those green eyes for exactly what it was, as well as the deathly pallor of her cheeks. 'I was in the theatre that night,' he added, so that there could be no doubts left in her mind as to exactly what he was talking about. 'The night of your accident.'

'No!' she protested weakly.

'Yes.' Darius nodded grimly, remembering clearly, as if in slow motion, watching the young ballerina on the stage as she seemed to stumble, attempt to stop herself from falling, before losing her balance completely and crashing down off the stage.

The whole audience had gasped, including Darius, followed by a hushed silence as the music and other dancers froze, and they all waited to know the extent of her injuries.

The realisation that she was the same Miranda Jacobs, the up-and-coming ballerina who had been lauded by the press and critics alike but had been forced to retire four years ago, following that aborted performance as Odette in *Swan Lake*, now explained so much about her.

That recognition Darius had when he looked at her, for one thing.

Her natural, almost ethereal slenderness, for another.

That fluidity of grace she possessed, just walking across a room. A gracefulness that was apparent in everything she did. Sitting, crossing her ankles, or lifting her champagne glass to her lips.

Everything about this woman was innately graceful.

Even the pained vulnerability he could now see in her eyes.

He had touched on a subject that so obviously caused her immense pain and distress.

Not surprising, when just four short years ago Miranda Jacobs had been called the Margot Fonteyn of her age. She had been an absolute joy to watch that night, mesmerisingly so. And that hadn't been just Darius's opinion, but also that of all the reviewers and the newspapers the following day as the headlines had delivered the news of the terrible accident on stage that might possibly mark the end of such a young and promising career.

That *had* been the end to Miranda Jacobs's

career as a professional ballet dancer; those same newspapers had reported just days later that her injuries were so extensive she would never dance professionally again.

Well, that might be true professionally...

Darius stood up abruptly before moving round the table and exerting a light pressure on Miranda's wrist as he pulled her to her feet beside him. 'Let's dance.'

Her expression was panicked as she pulled against that hold on her wrist. 'No.'

Darius stilled. 'Is there any medical reason that says you can't do a slow dance?'

Her eyes flashed a glittering emerald. 'I'm not a cripple, Mr Sterne, I'm just no longer capable of dancing in a professional capacity.'

'Then let's go.' His tone brooked no argument as he released her hand to instead place his arm firmly about the slenderness of her waist, holding her possessively into his side as he strode towards the dance floor, deliberately catching the eye of the DJ and giving the other man a barely perceptible nod of his head as he did so.

Mere seconds later the tempo of the music changed to a slow love song.

'That was convenient,' Miranda bit out abruptly as the two of them stepped onto the dance floor.

'No, actually, it was deliberate,' Darius dismissed unapologetically; he wanted this woman in his arms, and he wasn't about to pretend otherwise.

She gave a protesting shake of her head, the straight curtain of her hair moving about her shoulders as she placed her hands against his chest, with the obvious intention of pushing him away. 'I really don't want to dance.'

'Liar,' Darius stated arrogantly as he refused to release her; he had felt the increase of the pulse in her wrist, and his arms about her waist now allowed him to feel the fluttering of excitement that ran through the whole of her body. Very like that of a caged and wounded bird longing to be set free.

Damn it, he was starting to sound poetic again!

If nothing else, his mother's distant behaviour towards him these past twenty years had taught him that women were fickle and cold and not to be trusted with his feelings.

Nor did he become involved, in any way, with women who were complicated, or wounded, as Miranda Jacobs so obviously was. He carried around enough emotional baggage, the rest of his family's as well as his own, without taking on someone else's. Hell, he didn't become involved with women at all, except in the bedroom, and even then only on a purely sexual basis. Just a scratch to his itch.

But having forced the dancing issue he could hardly back down now. 'Move your feet, Miranda,' he encouraged huskily as he lifted her hands up onto his shoulders before pulling her closer still as he began to move slowly in time to the music, leaving Miranda with no choice but to follow his lead.

She was so slender in his arms that Darius almost felt as if he might bruise the willowy slenderness curved against his much larger and harder frame. And if he feared bruising her, just from dancing with her, how much more likely was it that he would completely crush her if he were to ever attempt to make love with her?

That was no longer even a possibility.

Making love to this woman was a definite no-no as far as Darius was concerned. Knowing who she was, who she had *been*, he also knew this woman was just too vulnerable, her past making her far too emotionally complicated, for him to even contemplate continuing his pursuit of the attraction he felt between the two of them. One dance together, and that was it. Then he would take her back to her booth, before returning to his office until she and the rest of her family had left the nightclub.

Never to return.

Yes, that was what he would do.

Her hair felt smooth as he rested his cheek lightly against it, those silver-gold tresses smelling of citrus and some deeper, enticing spice, that caused his hardened body to throb achingly as he breathed the scent deeply into his lungs. An arousal that Miranda, with the proximity of their two bodies, couldn't help but be completely aware of.

Andy was too disturbed at first, at finding herself dancing in public again, albeit in a crowded club, to be aware of anything else. But as her nerves slowly settled, and the trembling stopped, she couldn't help but become completely aware of the man she was dancing with.

She was five-eight in her bare feet, and even adding a couple of inches for the heels on her sandals Darius still towered over her by a good five or six inches. The width of his shoulders felt hard and muscled beneath her fingers. His chest and abdomen felt just as firmly muscled as he curved her body against and into his. As evidence, perhaps, that he didn't spend all of his time behind a desk counting his billions.

Well…no, she was sure that Darius spent a lot of energy exercising in his bedroom too. Horizontally!

None of which changed the fact that being so totally aware of the hardness of his thighs, and the heavy length of his arousal pressing against her contrasting softness, had completely taken her mind off the fact that she was actually dancing in public again. More of a shuffle, really, but it was still dancing.

And it was with Darius Sterne.

Darius had to be at least ten years older than her, as well as far more experienced and sophisticated. He was a man who no doubt changed the women in his bed as often as some minion changed the silk sheets for him afterwards, which would be often.

Andy already knew those silk sheets would be black—

Already knew?

Did that mean she was seriously imagining herself one day sharing Darius's bed sheets with him? Sharing his *bed*?

She hadn't needed to be in this man's company for two minutes to know that she should have heeded Kim's warning earlier. To know that Darius would eat her alive. Totally possess her. Devour her. Inch by fleshly inch. Bit by arousing bit!

The shiver that now coursed down Andy's spine was one of pleasurable anticipation. A longing, a yearning, for whatever Darius wanted to give her.

She couldn't do this.

No doubt other woman, so many other women, would be flattered just to have attracted the attention of a man like Darius. Even more so, to know that he had deliberately engineered her presence in the Midas club tonight, before he had swooped down on her, his arousal now unmistakeable as he danced so close against her.

Other women would be flattered.

Andy couldn't have the luxury of allowing herself to be flattered by the attentions of a man as dangerous as she considered Darius to be. Not when she knew it could ultimately lead nowhere.

Four years ago her dreams had been shattered. The dream she'd had since the age of five, of being a world-class ballerina, had come crashing down about her ears. Just as surely as she had come crashing down off the stage, shattering her hip and thigh bones.

It had taken over a year of operations and physical therapy for Andy to even be able to walk again, let alone be strong enough to rise up from beneath the misery threatening to bury her. But she had finally done it, had known she had no choice, that she needed to seriously consider her options for the future, now that she could no longer pursue her longed for career.

In the end she had realised that ballet was all she knew; she had won a scholarship to ballet school when she was eleven, had lived, eaten and breathed that world for so long, she couldn't imagine ever cutting herself off from it completely.

Opening up her own dance studio, while making her painfully aware of her own inadequacies, had seemed the natural solution.

Even that had taken hard work, and Andy had studied hard to take her teaching certificate, before just six months ago finally managing to open her own dance studio. She still had a long way to go for it to be as successful as she wanted it to be.

She certainly didn't have the time, or the emotional energy, to indulge in even a flirtation with a man like Darius. A man who she had no doubts broke women's hearts on a regular basis. A man who would have made no secret of the fact that none of those women had meant any more to him than just another conquest, a beautiful body to be enjoyed in his bed, and totally forgotten about the following morning.

Except Andy's body was no longer beautiful; how could it be, when it bore the physical scars from those many operations?

She pulled out of his arms the moment the song came to an end. 'As I said, thank you for inviting us all up here, and for the champagne and the dance.' She made her voice deliberately light, her smile bright and meaningless. 'Now, if you'll excuse me, I see that my sister and brother-in-law are waiting for me at the table, no doubt so that we can all leave,' she added wryly. Kim, at least, was glaring accusingly across the room at Darius.

He frowned. 'It's still early.'

'Maybe for you.' Andy nodded. 'Some of us have to get up for work in the morning.'

'Doing what?'

Her chin rose. 'I now own my own dance studio, teaching ballet to children. Yes,' she snapped as she saw his eyebrows rise, 'a typical example of "those that can't, teach"! Now, if you'll excuse me?'

'No!'

Andy looked up at him uncertainly as she heard vehemence in his tone. 'No?'

It was one thing for Darius to have decided

he couldn't take his attraction towards this woman any further than he already had, and quite another for Miranda to decide to walk away from him.

Damn it, had he really become so arrogant that he couldn't accept a woman's lack of interest in him for what it was?

Hell, yes, he was that arrogant!

Most especially when he knew that Miranda wasn't uninterested in him at all.

The sexual tension between the two of them had been palpable downstairs in the restaurant earlier, and it was even deeper now that they had actually talked, and then danced together.

'Have dinner with me tomorrow night,' Darius prompted abruptly as he turned to place a restraining hand on her arm before they could reach the table where her sister and brother-in-law were waiting for her.

'I— What—? No!' Miranda looked totally flustered by the invitation.

'Why on earth not?' He scowled darkly.

She gave an impatient shake of her head. 'As I said, I'm grateful to you for inviting us up to your club, and—and everything else. It's made my birthday even more special. I just— This— You and me— It isn't going anywhere.'

'I only invited you out to dinner, Miranda, not to become the mother of my children,' he pointed out dryly.

The colour had first drained and then deepened in her cheeks. 'And when was the last time you invited a woman out to dinner without the expectation of taking her to bed at the end of the evening?' Her pointed chin rose challengingly as she looked up at him.

'And what makes you so sure that isn't going to happen?' he purred.

Andy wasn't sure of anything in regard to her undeniable and unexpected attraction to this man; that was the problem!

It would be too easy to become completely caught up in Darius, in his mesmerising attractiveness, in that arrogance and certainty, only to have all of that crash down about her ears when he realised, when he *saw*, her physical imperfections.

Physical imperfections, scars, which she had no doubts would illicit either pity or disgust. And Andy wanted neither of those things from Darius.

'I said no, I won't have dinner with you tomorrow, Mr Sterne. Or any other time,' Andy added as she pointedly removed her arm from his grasp. 'Excuse me.' She didn't wait for a response from him this time as she turned and walked away determinedly.

As she turned and walked away from the man she knew, instinctively, was capable of capturing her heart before just as quickly breaking it.

CHAPTER THREE

'I THOUGHT I would wait for your students to leave before I came in.'

Andy froze as Darius Sterne's voice echoed across her otherwise empty dance studio, her gaze now riveted on the mirrored wall in front of her as she saw his reflection in the doorway behind her.

It had been a week since she had left him at Midas, and he looked as tall and darkly forbidding as ever. Today he wore a charcoal-coloured suit and paler grey shirt and tie, beneath a dark overcoat. The darkness of his hair was even longer than a week ago, and more tousled about those harshly patrician features, his topaz gaze fixed on her intently.

Andy's last class of the afternoon had just left and she was currently standing beside the barre on the wall going through the routine of exercises and stretches that she did at the end of each day, before going up to her apartment to shower and change.

What on earth was Darius even *doing here*?

How was he here at all? Andy didn't remember telling him where her dance studio was located, only that she had one.

He was Darius Sterne, and if he wanted to find out exactly where that dance studio was situated, then no doubt he could just instruct one of his employees to find out for him.

The real question was: *why* had he?

Andy had tried her best not to even think about this disturbing man for the past week. Or her unprecedented physical response to him!

And for the most part she knew that she had succeeded, spending the weekend either going out with Kim and Colin, or cleaning her flat, and keeping herself busy at her studio the rest of the time, as she kept thoughts of Darius at bay.

Unexpectedly hearing the husky sound of his voice, and just a single glance at his reflection in the mirror, and Andy knew she had been wasting her time trying so hard not to think about this man this past week. She could feel the moist heat gathering between her thighs, and her breasts were already tingling with arousal.

And those were the reasons Andy couldn't turn and face him, but instead continued to look at his reflection in the mirrored wall in front of her, her fingers now curled so tightly about the barre beside her that her knuckles showed white.

'I had to separate two of those little angels before class began; they were arguing over whose leotard was the prettiest,' she answered dryly.

'Women in the making,' he teased.

'No doubt,' Andy answered dismissively before asking the question she really wanted an answer to. 'What are you doing here, Mr Sterne?'

At this precise moment, Darius was exerting all of his considerable will power to control the urge he felt to quickly cross the studio and kiss her delectable lips, before baring her body and kissing that too!

Who knew that a woman could look so sexy in a leotard and tights?

That *Miranda Jacobs,* specifically, would look so sexy in a white leotard and tights, with silky white ballet shoes on her slender feet?

The long-sleeved leotard hugged every inch of her body, outlining her small but perfectly rounded breasts tipped with ripe—and aroused?—berries. His gaze took in her tiny waist, the slight flare of her hips, her bottom two perfectly rounded globes, her legs long and shapely in white tights. Her hair was brushed back and secured in a ponytail at her crown and her face, completely bare of make-up, tinged with a slight glow of warmth to her satiny smooth skin. No doubt the latter was from her recent exertions with the dozen or so small children that had just left with their doting mothers in tow.

He had his own driver, but had chosen to drive himself to the dance studio. He'd arrived about fifteen minutes ago, the amount of other vehicles in the car park telling him that she must have a class on at the moment. Sure enough, shortly after he'd parked his car, the young students had all trooped out and disappeared off with their mothers in their various vehicles and directions.

For some reason Darius hadn't expected that Miranda would be dressed in the same leotard and tights as her small charges wore. Or that it would take just one look at her in those revealing clothes for his body to harden to a painful throb!

It was a reaction that didn't improve his temper in the slightest; he had already thought about this young woman far more over this past week than he was happy with—in the middle of business meetings, on a couple of long flights, in the shower, *in his otherwise empty bed*!—without becoming aroused almost the moment he set eyes on her again.

'Mr Sterne?'

While he had been lost in the thought of exactly how and when he would like to have sex with her, Miranda had turned to face him, her head tilted curiously as those green and gold eyes looked across at him quizzically.

Miranda Jacobs was all and everything that Darius deliberately avoided in a woman.

And yet here he was, a week after their first meeting, hard and aroused after taking just one look at her.

Darius had tried taking out and bedding other women the past seven days—and nights —several of them to be exact. But every time it came to the end of the evening an image of ash-blonde hair and a willowy, desirable body would flash inside his head, totally deflating any desire he might feel to have sex with the woman he was with.

Every time he stepped into the shower, or climbed into bed at night, he could imagine that ash-blonde hair either slicked back and wet from taking a shower with him, or feathered out on his pillows, her green eyes sultry as she looked up at him invitingly, and making any idea of sleeping impossible. He also resented having to take care of his arousal himself.

He certainly didn't appreciate having had an image of Miranda popping into his head in the middle of a business meeting, as it had earlier this week in Beijing!

Something had to be done. And the only solution Darius could come up with was to take her to bed, before then putting her firmly from his mind.

If that meant he had to wine and dine Miranda, charm her—although that part might be a strain on his usual taciturn nature!—before then seducing her and taking her to his bed, then that was what Darius had decided he had to do. For his own sanity, if not hers.

His mouth thinned. 'I was under the impression you no longer danced?' He swept his gaze up and over her leotard once more.

'I dance enough to be able to demonstrate the moves to my students, and to be able to do that I need to dress as they do.' Andy was thankful that the thick white tights she was wearing also hid the mesh of scars on her right hip and thigh.

'So why are you here, Mr Sterne?'

He drew his breath in sharply. 'I came to invite you to attend a charity dinner with me on Saturday evening.'

To say Andy was surprised by the invitation would be putting it mildly.

Although she did know, after finally giving in and looking him up on the Internet, that Darius wasn't now, nor had he ever been, married, or even engaged to be married. In fact, at the age of thirty-three he had never been involved in a single serious relationship, as far as Andy could tell from the information available on him.

Which, surprisingly, hadn't been as detailed as she had expected it to be.

There had been plenty of articles on how successful he and his brother were in business; it appeared they owned *half* the known universe, not almost all of it, as she had first thought!

There were also numerous publicity photographs of him and his brother, and others taken of him at exotic locations all over the world, with beautiful and glamorous women on his arm. Noticeably the majority of those women had been tall and shapely brunettes.

But Darius Sterne's private life seemed to be exactly that: private.

Oh, on the surface of it there appeared to be plenty of details.

She'd discovered the names of the schools he had attended, followed by a degree at Oxford University. She'd read up on the social network site that had been the start of the successful business empire that he had owned with his twin brother for the past twelve years. As well, there had been a brief mention of the fact that his father had died when he was thirteen, and his mother had remarried when he was fourteen. But that was all it had been; there was nothing *tangible* about Darius himself. Nothing about Darius Sterne the man, or his relationship with the rest of his family, apart from that business partnership with his twin. And despite Kim's warnings of a lurid past—and present?—there had been no 'kiss and tell' newspaper articles from any women Darius might have scorned.

Although Andy suspected that the reason for the latter was because Darius either owned, or had influence over, most of the world's media.

She now also knew he lived mainly in a penthouse apartment in London, but also owned other homes in several capital cities around the world, including New York, Hong Kong, and Paris.

But again, none of those things were personal to the man.

After reading everything she could find that had ever been written on Darius, the only thing that Andy knew with any certainty was that she wasn't, in any way, shape or form, his type!

And yet here he surprisingly was, and asking her to go out with him again.

'Why?' She picked up a towel and draped it about the dampness of her neck and shoulders, making sure it also covered her breasts. Her cheeks warmed as she walked across the smooth wooden floor towards him. Thankfully, without any sign of the limp she sometimes developed when she was tired.

And how, Andy wondered irritably, considering that she was covered completely, did the intensity of Darius's gaze as he watched her approach somehow manage to make her feel as if she were naked from head to toe instead?

'Saturday is only two days away,' she taunted as she came to a halt just feet away from him. 'So did your original date have to cancel?'

Andy gave an inner wince even as she asked the question; if Darius Sterne's original date had cried off, for whatever reason, then there was a multitude of women who would happily have taken her place. He certainly didn't need to resort to going to the trouble of seeking Andy out, for the sole purpose of inviting her to go with him.

'I didn't have a previous date.' He raised dark brows, as the same thought obviously crossed his own mind. 'It is a bit short notice, I admit, but I only arrived back from a lengthy business trip at six o'clock this morning.'

'And no doubt you immediately thought of me!' she dismissed scathingly.

'What makes you think I ever stopped thinking of you?' he challenged.

Andy found it hard to believe that Darius had given her a single thought after their first meeting, especially when he seemed to have been out of the country for the past week.

And yet he was asking her to believe that just hours after his return he had come here to see her?

Andy was determined not to read too much into that. 'Arrived back from where?'

'China.'

'They don't have telephones in China?'

His jaw tightened at her sarcasm. 'You didn't give me your telephone number or email address.'

'I didn't give you the address of my dance studio either, but you don't seem to have had any trouble finding that out for yourself,' she countered.

His eyes glittered his displeasure at the underlying sarcasm in her voice. 'I thought you would prefer that I came here and made the invitation in person.'

'Did you?' Andy mused. 'Or did you imagine I might find it harder to refuse you in person?'

Darius had convinced himself this past week that Miranda Jacobs couldn't possibly be as intractable as he had thought she was being that night at his club. That maybe she had just been playing hard to get last week, in an effort to pique his interest. Just five minutes back in her infuriating company, and he knew that Miranda was every bit as stubborn as he had first thought she was.

He wasn't used to being told the word no, by any woman. Not once, but twice!

Darius slid his hands into the pockets of his suit trousers, rather than reach out and touch Miranda, not sure which would win out if he did touch her: his need to shake her or kiss her!

'You didn't seem to have any problem with saying no to me in person last week.'

She gave a shrug of those slender shoulders. 'Which begs the question, why are you bothering to ask me again, when you already know the answer?'

Darius breathed in sharply, his hands clenching in his trouser pockets, as he once again fought the need he felt to reach out and shake this woman. An impulse he resisted because he had every reason to believe he *would* then be tempted into kissing her. Senseless! 'I thought the charity benefitting from the dinner might be of interest to you,' he bit out between tightly clenched teeth.

Andy eyed him guardedly, very aware of the tension thrumming through Darius's lean and muscled body, as he now stood just inches away from her.

Of excited awareness thrumming through her own body.

Just as she was also aware of how alone they were in the studio, with only the distant noise of the traffic outside to disturb the tension between the two of them.

She gave a slow shake of her head. 'Why are you doing this, Darius?' she asked softly. 'What possible interest can you have in taking out a failed ballerina?'

'You didn't fail, damn it!' Darius cut in harshly, his brief elation at finally hearing her call him Darius having been completely overridden by the anger he now felt at hearing her describe herself as a failure.

Once he had accepted that his desire for Miranda wasn't going to go away, he had made it his business to find out all that he could about her.

And a failure wouldn't have fought and struggled her way back onto her feet after undergoing numerous operations, in the way that he now knew Miranda had needed to do four years ago.

A failure wouldn't have studied and worked so hard in the years since, in order to earn a teaching certificate in the subject she loved, but could no longer participate in herself.

A failure wouldn't have spent most of her share of the inheritance left to her and her sister by her parents five years ago to open up this dance studio.

The Internet truly was an intrusive thing…

Even if he had made the start of his fortune out of it!

And the ballerina Miranda Jacobs, and the tragic accident during her performance of *Swan Lake*, had once been part of that public domain. Not so much once she had begun her long recovery and disappeared from the newspaper headlines; stories in the tabloids were always fleeting, instant things, with none of those newspapers interested in reporting anything long-term.

Darius had his own method of finding out anything that he wanted to know. And, within days of meeting her, he had wanted to know everything there was to know about Miranda.

'I doubt you have ever failed at anything in your life,' he repeated.

'So you prefer we think of it as my just having made a career change?' she mocked. 'A step sideways, if you'll excuse the pun?'

'I prefer to think of it as you working with what you have left,' Darius dismissed briskly; annoying as Miranda was being, he was determined not to argue with her. 'So, about this dinner on Saturday?'

'You mentioned I might be interested in the charity?'

Darius masked his inner triumph as Miranda showed a grudging interest. 'It's in aid of disabled and underprivileged children.'

A charity that *did* interest her, Andy admitted irritably, and one she already worked with; she gave over one of her sessions a week to working with disabled and/or underprivileged children.

Had Darius already known that?

Of course he had. He was a man who would make it his business to know anything he wanted to know. And for some reason he had wanted to know about her.

Or maybe it was that he thought of *her* as some sort of charity? Someone who had once been in the public eye, but now lived and worked in obscurity, at her little dance studio in the suburbs of London?

'You know, Miranda, I was really hoping to do this the nice way.'

Andy looked up at him sharply. 'What does that mean?' She eyed him warily, not at all comfortable with that feral smile now curving those sculptured lips. It was not the genuine smile she had visualised last week, but nevertheless it still put two attractive grooves into the lean hardness of his cheeks.

'If you just say yes, to accompanying me to the charity dinner, then you'll never need to know.' He shrugged.

Andy's unease only increased at his pleasant tone. 'Could it possibly have anything to do with the fact that my brother-in-law works for you?' She had been very aware of that fact from the moment Darius had approached and spoken to her in the club last week. She just hadn't believed he would actually stoop to using that connection in order to impose his considerable will.

Until now.

'Intelligent as well as beautiful!' His smile was genuinely appreciative. 'Yes, my brother and I have been in several meetings this week, listening to our managers as they listed all the reasons why we no longer need such big IT departments in our offices around the world, most especially in London. A drop-in workforce is, I'm afraid, inevitable. It's just a question now of deciding who is or who isn't expendable.'

And they both knew that Colin worked in the IT department of the London offices of Midas Enterprises! 'That's despicable.' Andy was incredulous.

'I know,' Darius drawled. 'And I feel so bad about it,' he added insincerely.

Andy glared up at him, not sure if she wanted to punch him on his arrogant nose or just slap his face. Either way she knew it would give her only a fleeting sense of satisfaction. Nor was it an action that Darius would leave unpunished—and possibly by deciding that Colin was definitely expendable at Midas Enterprises.

'Colin is a real person, with financial responsibilities,' she snapped. 'He's not some toy you can play with just to get your own way.'

Darius shrugged. 'Then stop being difficult.'

She eyed him scathingly. 'Are you really so desperate to secure a date for Saturday evening that you would resort to blackmail?'

'I'm not desperate at all.' His humour had faded as quickly as it appeared, his eyes now hard, his mouth a thin, uncompromising line. 'And I don't want a date with just anyone, Miranda. I want a date with *you*.'

She eyed him impatiently. 'Is this because I said no to you last week? Because no woman is *allowed* to say no to the imperious Darius Sterne? Are you so arrogant, so full of your own importance, that—' Andy's insulting tirade was brought to an abrupt halt as she felt herself pulled effortlessly into Darius's arms before his mouth came crashing down to capture hers.

It was by no means a gentle or exploratory kiss; it was more like being swept along on a tidal wave as his mouth devoured hers, his arms about her waist moulding her softness against the hardness of his chest and thighs, as his tongue now stroked, caressed, the soft sensitivity of her parted lips, before plunging into the moist heat of her mouth.

Andy was totally overwhelmed by the onslaught of desire that coursed through her as her hands moved up his chest and grasped onto his shoulders, before her fingers became entangled in the silky dark thickness of hair at his nape as she moved up onto her toes to return the heat of that kiss.

She was totally aware of the sensitivity, the arousal of her breasts, as her engorged nipples rubbed against the abrasive material of his coat. Only the thin material of her leotard and Darius's trousers stood between the hardness of his thighs and the heat that now burned between her own thighs.

Darius was breathing hard when he finally broke the kiss, his eyes the colour of dark amber as he continued to hold her in his arms as he looked down at her. '*That's* the reason I'm willing to use blackmail in order to get you to agree to go to this dinner with me on Saturday evening.'

Andy felt light-headed as she gazed up at him, and she realised that was because she had forgotten to breathe for the duration of that punishing kiss. A kiss she inwardly acknowledged she hadn't wanted to end.

What was *wrong* with her? This man had been nothing but arrogant and pushy since she first met him. To the point that he was now trying to blackmail her into going out with him on Saturday evening, and using Colin's job as leverage to do so.

Damn it, she wasn't even sure she *liked* the man.

Did she have to like him in order to be aroused by him?

Obviously not, if the heat of desire that still consumed her was an indication.

She moistened her slightly bruised lips with the tip of her tongue before answering him, instantly wishing she hadn't, as she tasted Darius on her lips: a heady mixture of warm honey and desire. She gave a determined shake of her head in an effort to dispel the fog of desire that seemed to have taken over her brain. 'Will the press be there?'

'What?' Darius had absolutely no idea what she was talking about.

If he was honest, at the moment he had no idea what day of the week it was. Kissing Miranda had been so much *more* than he had been expecting. So much more *intense* than anything he had ever felt with any other woman.

She frowned. 'Will any of the press be there on Saturday evening?'

'Oh.' He nodded, his brows clearing. 'Only those officially invited by my mother.'

'Your *mother*?'

Darius slowly, reluctantly, released Miranda before stepping back.

Before he did something stupid, like kissing her again; just that once was enough to tell him that the desire he had been feeling for her this past week had been the tip of an iceberg.

That he wanted so much more from Miranda than just a kiss. And that now, when she was still so determined to resist him, as well as tired and hot from a long day at work, wasn't the right time for the long, slow seduction he had in mind.

Running his hand through the tousled thickness of his hair made him instantly recall the way Miranda's slender fingers had been entangled in it just minutes ago. 'It's one of my mother's pet charities,' he dismissed huskily. 'As president of that charity, she's also the main organiser.'

As far as Andy was concerned, this whole situation had become slightly surreal.

All of it. Darius's initial and unexpected appearance at her studio. His invitation to the charity dinner. His having resorted to using blackmail in order to force her into accepting that invitation. A charity dinner, Darius had now informed her, that was being organised by his own mother!

'Isn't introducing me to your mother a little too cosy and intimate for you?' Andy taunted to hide how disturbed she was from the kiss they had just shared. Her legs were still feeling slightly shaky, her breasts an aching, unfulfilled throb.

A reaction, an arousal, that warned her

against spending any more time in this man's company than she had to. That warned she certainly shouldn't agree to accompany him to this charity dinner on Saturday.

Except Andy already knew she was going to say yes.

Because Darius had blackmailed her into accepting?

Or was the real reason because she secretly wanted to go out with him on Saturday evening, and it was just easier and less complicated—and less of a challenge to her inner warnings to do the opposite—to let Darius continue thinking she was only agreeing to go out with him because he had forced her to do so?

Andy had the next forty-eight hours, until she saw Darius again, to decide which of those it was.

Although she had a feeling she already knew the answer to that question.

She had been mesmerised by this man from the moment she first looked at him across the restaurant a week ago, even more so later that evening when he came over and spoke to her in the club, before insisting she danced with him. Since then Andy knew she hadn't been able to get Darius, and the sexual magnetism he exuded so confidently, out of her mind.

Despite all her efforts to the contrary.

She felt that magnetism all the deeper now that he had kissed her.

Darius now gave a scathing snort. 'There is nothing in the least cosy or intimate about my mother!'

Andy looked up at him searchingly as she heard the harshness of his tone. A curiosity Darius met with a blank stare, his eyes giving away none of his inner thoughts or emotions, just as the blandness of his expression revealed none of his outer ones, either.

She gave a grimace. 'You obviously don't really want to go to the dinner either, so why bother going?'

Darius looked away, only to be bombarded with dozens of reflections of the two of them from the mirrored walls, he standing tall and dark before a much slighter and fairer Miranda.

His breath caught in his throat as he imagined making love to Miranda in this room, with those same dozens of reflections, the two of them naked, reflected back at him. How much of a turn-on was just the thought of that? Enough so that his body hardened painfully.

He could easily imagine the two of them together here, knew that those multiple reflections would push his desire for Miranda to overload as he watched and enjoyed the two of them making love together.

He visualised the two of them, completely naked, as he stood behind Miranda, her silky, luminescent flesh very pale against his more olive skin as they stood close enough to the mirrors for him to see every nuance of expression on her face, but far enough away to ensure those multiple reflections.

His arousal would be pressed between the delicious globes of her bottom as he cupped her breasts in his hands, listening to her groans of pleasure as he played with and caressed her nipples, until they stood proud and full, and aching for more. Then he would move his hands lower, fingers splayed possessively across the flatness of her stomach, before moving down to allow his fingers to part the pale curls between her thighs and reveal the bud beneath, a bud that would be so aroused it would peep visibly from beneath its hood.

And then he would watch, would feast his eyes on that swollen nubbin as his fingers stroked and caressed. Would watch Miranda's silken thighs part as she allowed him greater access, pressing into his caressing fingers as she gasped her climax.

Then Darius would go on his knees in front

of her, greedily licking and caressing her to another orgasm.

And then again, and again.

He wanted to be able to watch that reflection as he parted her thighs before thrusting his length into her. To see how wet and swollen she was for him, a silken glove as she took all of him inside her, before he began to thrust into her, time and time again. And he would watch the ecstasy on Miranda's face as she climaxed for him again, before allowing himself to fall over that edge of pleasure with her.

He straightened abruptly. 'This particular charity dinner is a family obligation thing.'

'Really?' Miranda still eyed him curiously. 'You've never given me the impression you particularly care what anyone else thinks of you.'

'I don't,' he confirmed tersely. 'This is just — My mother throws one of these events once a year to celebrate her birthday, okay?' he bit out impatiently. 'Her private celebration was the reason the family was at the restaurant last Thursday.'

Did that mean that Catherine Latimer's birthday was on the same day as Andy's own?

Considering the tension she had picked up from Darius just now, when he spoke of his mother, the same tension she had sensed at the family dinner table last Thursday, not to mention the scowl Darius had given later on in the club when she had told him they were celebrating her own birthday, Andy had a feeling that it was…

Darius now gave an impatient glance at the gold watch fastened about his wrist. 'I have another appointment now, but I'll pick you up at seven-thirty on Saturday evening.'

Andy knew it was a statement rather than a request. A fait accompli, as far as Darius was concerned.

And maybe it was?

That less than subtle threat to Colin's job aside, didn't Andy *want* to accept Darius's invitation? Hadn't the curiosity she felt, for and about him, only increased after the passionate kiss they had just shared? So much so that Andy now *wanted* to see him again on Saturday evening?

The ache of her breasts and the dampness between her thighs said that she did. Even so…

'Don't think, just because I'm agreeing to go with you to this dinner on Saturday, that I'll allow you to blackmail me into doing anything else,' she warned challengingly. 'I love my brother-in-law dearly, but this is most definitely a one-off thing!'

Darius raised teasing brows. 'Maybe I won't need to use blackmail in order to get you to do anything else?'

Andy's lips thinned at his mockery.

'I'm afraid you'll never know—because I have no intention of seeing you again after Saturday night,' she countered with insincere sweetness.

Only to then catch her breath in her throat as Darius laughed. It was a slightly gruff sound, as if he really were out of practice. At the same time as he looked just as good as Andy had suspected he might…

His eyes glowed a deep, molten gold, laughter lines fanning out from beside them, those attractive grooves in the hardness of his cheeks making another appearance, his teeth very white and straight against those chiselled lips.

Darius was *breathtaking* when he laughed.

It was a laughter that faded, all too quickly for Andy's liking, to a derisive smile that became mocking. 'Maybe after Saturday night I won't need to blackmail you into seeing me again.'

'And maybe after Saturday night you won't *want* to see me again!' Andy ignored the innuendo as she answered him challengingly.

Darius became very still as he saw as well as

heard that challenge, in the deep green of Miranda's eyes and her defiant stance. 'I would advise that you don't deliberately do or say anything to embarrass me on Saturday evening.'

She raised innocent brows. 'I don't know you well enough to know what would embarrass you!'

'I can't think of anything offhand,' Darius drawled dismissively.

'That's what I thought,' she came back pertly. 'I live in the apartment above here. But then you already know that, don't you?' she stated impatiently as he raised a knowing eyebrow. 'Okay. Fine. Seven-thirty on Saturday evening.'

Darius might not have experienced it for a long, long time—if at all!—but he nevertheless knew when he was being dismissed.

Still, it was a dismissal he was prepared to allow for the moment, when he knew that staying here any longer would put him in serious jeopardy of forgetting his earlier decision to wait until Saturday before making love to Miranda.

'Saturday.' He lightly cupped her cheek as he bent and brushed a light kiss across her slightly parted lips. 'I'm looking forward to it already,' he murmured as he gazed down at her intently.

'I'm not!' Green eyes returned that gaze defiantly.

Darius found himself laughing again as he straightened before turning to leave. 'Don't forget to lock up after me,' he instructed as he reached the doorway, closing the door quietly behind him as he left.

He couldn't remember the last time a woman had made him laugh, let alone at the same time as his body was hard and throbbing with the desire to make love to her.

He couldn't remember the last time a woman had made him laugh at all.

In truth, he couldn't remember the last time he had genuinely laughed at anything…

CHAPTER FOUR

'JUST SMILE AND leave the talking to me,' Darius advised Andy softly on Saturday evening as the two of them moved steadily down the greeting line with the other glamorously clothed and bejewelled guests arriving at the London Midas Hotel for the charity dinner.

'Is that all your women are usually required to do?' Andy responded with brittle sweetness.

He raised dark brows. 'I'm going to ignore that remark, and put it down to nervousness on your part.'

Andy *was* nervous. And that nervousness was increasing the closer they came to where Darius's mother and stepfather, and presumably other members of the charity's committee, were personally greeting all the guests as they arrived.

She had spent most of the last forty-eight hours having second, third and *fourth* thoughts about the wisdom of seeing Darius again, when she so obviously had such a visceral response to him.

It was an uncharacteristic physical response, to any man, let alone one as dangerous as she considered Darius to be.

And considering her lack of experience in regard to men, she should probably have just dipped her toes gently in the water first, rather than jumping straight into the shark tank.

Especially when Darius was looking so tall, dark, and elegantly intimidating this evening, in his perfectly tailored black dinner jacket.

So much so that he had taken Andy's breath away when she'd opened the door of her apartment to him earlier.

Once again she had forgotten, or tried to forget in the last couple of days, just how *immediate* he was; so tall that he towered over her, his shoulders so broad they almost filled the doorway, his hair shorter than when she had last seen him, but still as tousled, as if he had been running his hands through it earlier.

Perhaps an indication that he was as nervous about seeing her again this evening as she was about seeing him?

Although Andy somehow doubted that!

Darius was always supremely confident, of himself, and other people's reaction to him.

Andy had hoped she hadn't given any indication of her nervousness earlier at her apartment as she'd calmly collected her jacket and clutch bag before following him outside, her fingers shaking slightly as she locked the door behind her.

The luxury car parked outside was a bit of a shock, but Andy felt she had behaved with poise when Darius had opened the door for her to get in before closing the door and moving round the car to sit behind the wheel.

She had also been quite proud of the fact that she had managed to keep up a light, impersonal conversation on the drive to the hotel. Despite the fact that she was so totally aware of the man seated beside her; of the lean strength of Darius's body, and the heady smell of healthy male and a lemon-based cologne.

But now that she was actually at the hotel where the charity dinner was being held, surrounded by the laughing and chattering rich and the famous, Andy knew she should have given more thought to how she was going to feel when she got here, rather than just focusing on seeing and being with Darius again,

Once upon a time she had occasionally stepped onto the edge of this glamorous world, when she had attended several of the after-gala performances of the ballet company. But she'd had a role on those occasions. A purpose. She had been an ambassador for the ballet company, rather than herself.

Here and now, Andy was merely an adjunct of Darius Sterne, and as such she was very aware of the curious glances that had come their way since they first entered the hotel together.

As aware as she was of the hand that Darius had placed possessively against her spine as they'd entered the hotel.

She was so aware that she was now able to feel the warmth of Darius's splayed fingers through the thin material of her black gown.

Andy had debated long and hard about what to wear this evening, and had gone through the contents of her wardrobe several times. She'd finally decided on a simple long black Grecian-style gown she had owned before the accident, but it was so classical in style it was dateless.

The gown left her arms and one of her shoulders bare, falling smoothly all the way to her ankles, the slit on the right side only going as far as her knee, and ensuring that the scars on her thigh wouldn't be visible even when she sat down. A requirement of all the clothes Andy had worn since the accident.

In keeping with the style of the gown, she had secured her hair loosely on her crown, leaving soft curls to cascade down onto her nape. Her make-up was light, just some dark shadow and mascara, and a deep peach lip gloss.

Andy had felt pleased with her appearance when she'd studied her reflection in the mirror before Darius arrived at her apartment. Here, amongst all these glamorous and beautiful women—several of whom were eyeing Darius as if they would like to devour him rather than the forthcoming dinner!—she felt less confident.

'I wouldn't have needed to *be* nervous at all if you hadn't used emotional blackmail to force me into coming here with you.' Andy made her point cuttingly.

Darius gave a humourless smile. 'Are you going to keep throwing that in my face all evening?'

'You can depend on it!' Her eyes flashed.

He gave an unconcerned shrug. 'I use whatever means I deem necessary at the time.'

'In order to get your own way.'

'Yes,' he confirmed unapologetically.

'Will your brother be here too this evening?' Andy decided to change the subject before the two of them ended up having a heated argument in front of all the other guests! Well, it would be heated on her part. Darius gave the impression that not too much penetrated that cool shield he kept about his emotions.

A façade that was instantly shattered as Darius looked down at her between narrowed lids. 'Why?'

'No particular reason.' She frowned at his sudden aggression. 'I was just changing the conversation to something less controversial.'

And Darius was *just* behaving like a jealous fool, he realised belatedly. Miranda had asked a perfectly polite question about his brother, and he had reacted like a Neanderthal.

Maybe it was the fact that she looked so stunningly beautiful tonight. Her figure-hugging gown was simply cut in comparison with the evening gowns worn by the other women present this evening, and styled in such a way that Darius could see she wasn't wearing a bra. She wore no jewellery at all, and very little make-up. The whole effect gave her the elegance of a swan in a roomful of peacocks.

Several male heads had turned Miranda's way when they'd entered the hotel together. Several of those men had continued to watch her covetously, until Darius had given each and every one of them a challenging glare.

To Miranda's credit she seemed totally unaware of that male interest.

As she seemed totally unaware of her own beauty.

Which was a novelty in itself.

Darius had never yet met a beautiful woman who wasn't totally aware of her own attractiveness, and what it could get her.

'I'm sure Xander will already be in the room somewhere,' he confirmed abruptly. 'Unlike me, he tries to cater to my mother's dislike of tardiness.'

Miranda gazed up at him curiously. 'One day you really will have to tell me what the problem is between you and your mother—' She stopped abruptly, a blush colouring her cheeks, because she had realised as soon as she said it that her mention of 'one day' implied she thought the two of them would be meeting again after this evening.

Darius smiled humourlessly. 'Oh, I really won't, angel,' he drawled dismissively.

'No. Well. Perhaps not,' Andy accepted awkwardly, the warmth having deepened in her cheeks at Darius's endearment. Unless he called all of his women *angel*? It would certainly save him any embarrassment if he forgot which woman he was spending the evening or night with.

Darius eyed her curiously. 'Did you tell your sister and brother-in-law that you were coming out with me this evening? Obviously not,' he drawled dryly as a guilty blush deepened the colour in Andy's cheeks.

'I couldn't think of an acceptable way to explain *why* the two of us had even met again, let alone that we were going out together,' she answered impatiently.

If she had even told Kim that Darius had visited her at her dance studio on Thursday, then heZr sister would have launched into yet another major big-sister lecture.

If Kim knew Darius had actually blackmailed Andy into going out with him this evening, and used Colin's continued employment for Midas Enterprises as leverage, then Andy had absolutely no doubts her sister wouldn't have hesitated in stating that Darius could do whatever the hell he pleased in that regard, because Andy wasn't going anywhere with him. Tonight or ever!

That was the excuse Andy gave herself for remaining silent on the subject, at least.

'You certainly wouldn't have come out of that explanation in a very good light,' Andy assured Darius.

He raised dark brows. 'And do you somehow have the mistaken idea that would actually have bothered me?'

'Obviously not,' she snapped her impatience. Honestly, what was wrong with this man? She had done as he'd asked, and come out to this dinner with him, so why was he now being so aggressive? 'Do you usually bring a date to one of these dinners?' She decided to attack rather than keep being put on the defensive. As she so often was where Darius was concerned.

But also because she knew, in her heart of hearts, that Kim would have been right to warn her off the man.

Being here with Darius *was* dangerous. *He* was dangerous to the ordered life Andy had painstakingly Zcarved out for herself these past four years.

Darius grimaced at her question. 'Never.'

Her eyes widened. 'Seriously?'

He gave a half-smile. 'Seriously.'

Oh, wonderful! Not only was she here with the most impressively handsome man in the room, and about to be introduced to his parents, but now she learnt that Darius usually attended these functions alone.

No wonder so many of the other guests, most especially the women, had stared at the two of them when they arrived. And were still staring at them.

Andy eyed him impatiently. 'Why now?'

'Wrong question, Miranda,' Darius bent

to murmur huskily against her ear as they approached the front of the line. 'The question should have been, Why *you*? Not, "Why now?"' he supplied huskily as Andy gave him a questioning glance.

Indeed, why her? Andy wondered dazedly —a question she was prevented from asking out loud as they finally stepped forward to be greeted by his parents.

'Miranda, Catherine and Charles Latimer,' Darius introduced with terse economy. 'Mother, Charles, this is Miranda Jacobs.' The last was accompanied by a challenging look at the older couple.

Catherine seemed momentarily disconcerted as her frowning gaze moved quickly to Miranda and then back at Darius. 'I wasn't aware you had purchased a second ticket for this evening.'

He raised dark, challenging brows. 'And I wasn't aware I needed your permission to do so.'

'Lovely to meet you, my dear.' Charles Latimer stepped into the awkward breach between mother and son, as if it was a habit of long standing. He was a white-haired and still handsome man. 'And so good of you to come along and support such a worthwhile charity.'

'Oh. Yes. Very kind of you.' Catherine belatedly remembered her manners, her smile tense as she offered her hand.

It was impossible for Andy not to be aware of the tension between mother and son. A tension that now seemed to include her.

'Mrs Latimer,' she returned lightly as the two women briefly shook hands. 'I hope it's a successful evening for you.'

'I hope so too.' Up close, it was impossible to miss the fine lines beside Catherine Latimer's eyes and mouth, as indication of her age, but she was nevertheless still a very beautiful woman, very slender and chic in her black designer-label evening gown; she certainly didn't look old enough to be the mother of thirty-something twins.

'Is Xander here?' Darius enquired abruptly.

'Not yet.' Catherine Latimer frowned. 'It's most unlike him to be late, I do hope nothing has happened to him,' she added with concern.

Darius's mouth twisted derisively. 'He's a big boy now, Mother. I'm sure he'll find his way here eventually.' He didn't wait for a response from either of the older couple, his expression grim as he placed a hand beneath Andy's elbow before turning her and walking away and into the crowd.

'That was incredibly rude of you,' Andy

muttered once they were out of earshot of the older couple.

Darius gave another unconcerned shrug. 'I thought you would have realised by now; I'm an incredibly rude man.'

No, actually, he wasn't.

Arrogant? Yes. Overbearing? Certainly. Blunt? Disconcertingly so. Ruthless, even— Darius's threats regarding Colin's job in order to force Andy into coming here with him this evening certainly came under the latter category! But Andy had never thought of Darius as being particularly rude.

Until he spoke of or to his mother.

There was definitely a story there. One which Darius had made it clear he had no intention of confiding in Andy. Because he wasn't a man who confided in anyone except perhaps his twin brother? Andy recalled that the brothers had arrived at the restaurant together last week, and they had been in business together for twelve years, so it was probably safe to assume they at least liked each other and got along.

'Is there some reason why your mother should be worried about Xander's lateness?' she prompted slowly.

Darius looked down at her coolly. 'None at

all—apart from the fact that she's overprotective of him to the point of obsession.'

An image of Darius's twin instantly came to mind: the golden-haired god with laughter in his dark eyes. 'Does she have reason to believe he's in need of protection?'

Darius breathed his impatience. 'You seem overly concerned with the non-appearance of my brother.'

Andy frowned at the accusation. 'Not in the least.'

'No?'

'No!'

Andy decided, with Darius looking so grimly unappreciative of this subject, that it might be best to talk of something less controversial.

'What I am curious to know is just how much the tickets cost for this dinner.'

There must be at least five hundred people in this crowded ballroom, all of them dressed in glamorous evening wear; the men all looked very distinguished in their black dinner suits, and the array of ladies' ballgowns was exquisite. Andy was in danger of being blinded by the amount of jewellery glittering beneath the crystal chandeliers.

Darius took two glasses of champagne from

one of the circulating waiters before handing one to Andy. 'Does it matter?'

'Only if it would be a complete waste of my time offering to pay for my own ticket!'

'It would,' Darius confirmed dryly.

'Oh.' She grimaced before taking a sip of her champagne; she knew that the tickets for some of these charity events cost in the thousands of pounds rather than the hundreds. And this evening looked to be one of the former.

'Not only would it be a waste of your time from a financial angle,' Darius continued dismissively, 'but also totally unacceptable. *I* was the one who invited *you* this evening; I doubt you would have come here of your own volition!'

Andy gave him a pointed glance. 'We both know that I didn't.'

He sighed heavily.. 'You really meant it when you said you aren't going to let that go, didn't you?'

'I really did,' she confirmed dryly. 'Do you think—?'

'Andy, is that you? My goodness, it *is* you!'

Andy had been so sure that she wouldn't know anyone else here this evening, and she now turned to look blankly at the woman who had just greeted her so enthusiastically. She looked at a tall and willowy brunette, dressed in a red sequinned dress that finished at least six inches above her shapely knees.

She was exactly the type of woman, tall and brunette, Andy had seen Darius photographed with so much in the past.

The woman had now moved forward to clasp one of Andy's hands in her own red-tipped ones, a smile tilting the edges of perfectly painted red lips. A smile that didn't reach the coldness of her blue eyes.

Andy's heart had sunk as she'd recognised Tia Bellamy, a member of the ballet company she had also belonged to so briefly four years ago. Tia was two years older than Andy, and had never been a particular friend of hers. She certainly hadn't been this friendly when the two of them worked together all those years ago.

'Tia,' she greeted stiffly, even as she removed her hand from the older woman's cooler one. 'How are you?'

Tia's smile widened. 'I'm currently in rehearsal for the lead in *Giselle*,' she announced with satisfaction, her gaze triumphant as she looked at Andy.

'Congratulations.' The smile remained fixed on Andy's face; she might have distanced herself from her previous life in ballet, but even she knew that during this past four years Tia had risen to the heights in the ballet company that she had always dreamed of reaching, that the other woman was now the company's principal dancer.

'You're looking absolutely marvellous,' Tia gushed insincerely. 'But you always did look good in this gown.' She gave Andy's ankle-length gown a knowing glance. 'Of course, I don't suppose you have any choice nowadays but to wear gowns that reach down to your ankles.'

Yes, Tia was still every bit as catty and competitive as she had always been; Andy had worn this gown *once* when they had known each other four years ago. Once!

And trust Tia to bring up the accident so quickly.

'Someone...I can't remember who...mentioned that you had opened a little dance studio or something now that you can no longer dance yourself,' Tia continued offhandedly.

'Yes,' Andy confirmed stiffly, not absolutely sure why she was even continuing this conversation when what she really wanted to do was just walk away—before she said something both women would regret.

'And is that going well for you?' Tia prompted with a continued lack of interest.

'Very well, thank you,' Andy answered abruptly.

'I'm so glad!' Tia dismissed in a bored voice before she turned to look up at Darius with flirtatious and covetous blue eyes. 'Aren't you going to introduce me, Andy?'

Given a choice, the answer to that question would be a resounding no. Andy had no interest in introducing Tia to Darius. She had no interest in Tia, full stop. As the other woman had made it obvious she had no interest in her either.

It was more than obvious, from the way Tia was now eyeing Darius, that meeting him was the real reason she had bothered to speak to Andy at all.

'Tia Bellamy...Darius Sterne.' Andy introduced him as abruptly as Darius had introduced her to his parents earlier.

'Mr Sterne, it's such a pleasure to meet you!' Tia purred throatily, her eagerness showing that she had known exactly who he was from the outset.

It had become obvious to Darius, from listening to their conversation, that the two women had once danced professionally together. That Tia Bellamy still danced.

It was also obvious that Ms Bellamy was being incredibly rude and hurtful for reminding Miranda so openly that she no longer could.

Just as it was also obvious, from the stiffness of Miranda's demeanour, the pallor of her cheeks, and the slight trembling of the hand that held her champagne glass, that this unexpected meeting with Tia Bellamy was not a welcome one for her.

Nor did Darius particularly care for the way in which the brunette was now eyeing him as if he were a particularly tasty snack. Not that it was the first time he had been ogled in this way—far from it; his wealth had always been more than enough incentive to produce this sort of reaction from a certain type of woman. But he considered it to be in exceedingly bad taste, when he was so obviously here with Miranda, and Tia Bellamy was pretending to be her friend.

A pretence he could only assume had to be for his benefit rather than anyone else's.

Because any real friend of Miranda's wouldn't have instantly boasted of dancing the lead in *Giselle*. Nor would they have asked so condescendingly about the dance studio Miranda had opened now that she was no longer able to dance professionally.

He was also curious to know what the other woman had meant when she commented that

Miranda had no choice but to wear gowns down to her ankles nowadays. What the hell did Tia Bellamy mean by that? Did Miranda actually have lasting physical scars from her accident four years ago, rather than just the emotional ones?

'Ms Bellamy.' Darius nodded tersely as he ignored the hand she held out to him and instead placed his free arm about the slenderness of Miranda's waist, a frown appearing between his eyes as he instantly felt the trembling of her body. He wasn't sure whether it was from anger or because she was upset. 'Please don't let us keep you from your date any longer,' he added dismissively, with a pointed glance at the middle-aged man hovering in the background.

'Oh, that's just Johnny—Lord John Smythe, you know—not my husband.' She turned to give the waiting man a sugary sweet smile. 'He's rather sweet, and he will keep proposing, but I certainly have no intention of accepting.' She gave Darius a flirtatiously coy smile that implied she would definitely accept a proposal from *him*.

Any proposal he cared to make.

An invitation Darius wouldn't have accepted even if he hadn't disliked the way she spoke to Miranda; Tia Bellamy was just like all those other beautiful women who saw him as nothing more than a wealthy meal ticket. 'You'll have to excuse us, Miss Bellamy, my brother has just arrived. Ready, angel?' His voice softened huskily as he looked down at Miranda.

She had been staring at Tia Bellamy as if mesmerised—or repelled?—and Darius now felt the shudder that ran through her body as she pulled herself together with effort.

'So nice to have seen you again, Tia.' Miranda's tone was as stiltedly polite as the other woman's had been falsely warm. 'If you'll excuse us?'

Darius's arm remained firmly about Miranda's waist as the two of them walked away. 'I take it there's some sort of history between the two of you?' he prompted gently once they were safely out of earshot of the other woman.

Andy drew in a shuddering breath, knowing that Darius was far too astute, too intelligent, not to have picked up on her tension as she'd forced herself to speak to the blasted woman.

Her first evening out in forever, and she had to meet the one woman she had hoped never to set eyes on again!

Not that she had thought for a moment that it had been an accidental meeting; Tia had made it obvious that she had deliberately made a point of seeking her out to get to Darius.

'Something like that,' Andy answered Darius dismissively.

'Care to talk about it?'

'No. I thought you said we were going to say hello to your brother,' she prompted in alarm as Darius took the champagne glass out of her hand and placed it with his own on a table, his arm about her waist anchoring her firmly to his side as he guided her out of the crowded and noisy ballroom, before striding purposefully down the hallway and then turning left down a deserted corridor of closed doors.

He didn't answer her as he stopped to open several of those doors before pushing one open into what turned out to be a small—and empty—conference room. He pushed Andy inside and closed the door behind them, instantly shutting out all other noise but the sound of the two of them breathing.

'I lied about seeing Xander,' Darius finally murmured as he leant back against the closed door, arms crossed in front of his chest, his gaze fixed on Andy intently as he effectively blocked her exit.

Andy's eyes widened. 'You seem to do that a lot.'

'On the contrary, I'm usually brutally honest.' He smiled.

But his smile held no warmth. 'Exactly who is Tia Bellamy, and why did meeting her again upset you so much?'

Well, that was certainly brutally honest enough, Andy acknowledged ruefully. Even if she had no intention of satisfying Darius's curiosity. 'We really should go back and join the other guests in the ballroom.'

'We really shouldn't,' Darius murmured huskily as he moved away from the door. 'Not until you've answered my question,' he added grimly.

'Which one?' She raised her chin challengingly.

His eyes glittered down at her just as determinedly as Darius shrugged. 'I believe they were one and the same question.'

'No, they weren't.' Andy sighed as she turned away to stand nearer the conference table, having known by the stubborn set of Darius's jaw that she wasn't about to escape this room until he was ready for the two of them to leave. 'Obviously Tia is a ballet dancer,' she dismissed. 'I'm surprised you haven't heard of her?' Andy had avoided looking at any newspaper articles or other ballet gossip since the accident, but even she knew that Tia was now one of England's prima ballerinas.

As she had once hoped to be.

'Business pressures mean I haven't had time to go to the ballet for years,' Darius dismissed. 'Now tell me why seeing her again upset you so much,' he insisted determinedly.

Andy shrugged as she turned away from his probing gaze. 'Surely it's only natural for me to be a little upset at seeing one of my old colleagues, and to be reminded of—of the fact that I'll never dance professionally again?'

'Now tell me the real reason.'

Andy knew, from how close Darius's voice was, and from the way his breath ruffled the soft downy hair at her nape, that he had crossed the room and was now standing just behind her.

So close to her, in fact, that Andy could feel the warmth of his body through the material of her gown, his unique and intoxicating smell—warm, virile male and that lemon-based cologne—invading her senses.

'Talk to me,' he prompted huskily.

Andy gave a shake of her head, in an effort to stop herself from falling any deeper under Darius's seductive spell.

'Tell me the real reason seeing Tia Bellamy upset you.' His voice had hardened.

She tensed. 'I already have.'

'No.'

'Yes.'

Andy realised it had been a mistake to turn and face Darius as she suddenly found herself pressed flush against the hardness of his body as he easily pulled her into his arms.

A move she attempted to resist at first, only to capitulate with a sigh, and rest her head against the solidity of his shoulder, when Darius simply refused to release her but instead tightened his arms about her in order to prevent her escape.

'Tell me,' he encouraged gruffly as he rested his cheek lightly against her hair.

That was something Andy couldn't do. Something she would never tell anyone ever again. She had tried four years ago to tell people what she thought had really happened the night she went tumbling down off the stage, smashing her right hip and thigh bone and effectively ending her ballet career. No one had believed her. No one had wanted to believe her.

In the end Andy hadn't been sure that she believed it herself either.

Admittedly Tia had been her understudy for the Odette/Odile role in *Swan Lake*, and had immediately taken over after Andy's accident, but she couldn't really have pushed Andy deliberately, in order to achieve that ambition. Could she?

Andy had convinced herself in the months of surgery and convalescence that had followed her accident that the events of that night must all have become muddled in her mind. That it had been the initial pain, and then the strong drugs they had given her to dull that pain, that had caused some sort of delirium, resulting in the weird dreams she had just thought were real when she woke up.

Tia's almost triumphant air this evening, when she'd announced she was rehearsing for the lead in *Giselle*, her condescension about the way Andy looked and was dressed this evening, her pitying glances when she mentioned Andy's dance studio, now caused Andy to once again question her memories of that night four years ago.

CHAPTER FIVE

ANDY MOISTENED THE dryness of her lips before answering Darius. 'I'll make a deal with you,' she murmured huskily. 'I'll answer your question if you'll tell me the reason for the friction between you and your mother.'

Darius gave a rueful chuckle. Miranda might have been shaken by that meeting with Tia Bellamy, but not so much that she couldn't think logically enough to ask him for the one thing she knew he couldn't, or rather wouldn't, give her. 'We both know that isn't going to happen.'

She gave a shrug. 'Then neither is my answer to your own question.'

Darius moved his head back slightly so that he could look down at her as he murmured appreciatively, 'You are one very dangerous lady.'

Miranda's eyes glowed with mischievous humour. 'I don't think anyone has ever accused me of being *that* before.'

Darius sobered as he looked down into the beauty of Miranda's face: those warm green eyes, her flushed cheeks, the full and tempting pout of her lips. Yes, to him, at this moment, she was most definitely very dangerous. 'Maybe that's because no one else has ever been as determined as I am to know you better?'

'Or in the way in which you want to know me better?' Andy countered ruefully.

Darius quirked one dark brow. 'Is that a bad thing?'

It wasn't 'bad' exactly—the intensity of desire Andy could see in Darius's eyes just scared the hell out of her.

It didn't help that Andy was so aware of his body pressed so intimately against her own. Or how alone they were in this room. She certainly couldn't dismiss the sexual tension that now surrounded the two of them, and appeared to hold both of them in its thrall.

Which, considering there were five hundred people in the huge ballroom just a short distance away, was totally inappropriate.

'What did Tia Bellamy mean when she said you need to wear long gowns, Miranda?' Darius asked unexpectedly.

So unexpectedly that Andy felt her cheeks pale. 'That's none of your business, Darius.'

'I'm making it so,' he insisted softly.

Andy shook her head in denial. 'I think we should go back to the ballroom now.'

'I disagree.'

'I don't care.'

'If I stop asking questions will you agree to stay here a little longer?' Darius leant back against the conference table and took Andy's bag from her unresisting fingers and placed it on the table behind him. He settled her in between his parted legs, his arms light about her waist as his lips nuzzled and tasted the warmth of her throat.

Much as she knew she shouldn't, Andy wanted nothing more than to stay here with Darius. And not just because she had no wish to bump into Tia Bellamy again, or engage in more conversation with Darius's family.

She had been physically aware of Darius since the moment he'd arrived at her apartment earlier this evening, and that awareness had only deepened as they'd sat in the warm confines of his car, and become even greater when Darius first placed, and then kept that possessive hand pressed against her spine as they'd entered the hotel together.

Alone with him now, just the two of them in the silence of this conference room, Darius's lips a warm and arousing caress against the column of her throat, Andy had absolutely no defences against the heat of desire warming and spreading through the whole of her body. Nor could she deny that now familiar full feeling in her breasts, her nipples incredibly sensitive as they rubbed against Darius's jacket, her thighs perfectly aligned with his as he leant back against the conference table, allowing her to feel the long hard ridge of his arousal.

'Are you wearing anything at all beneath this gown?' Darius's lips had now travelled down to where one of his hands cupped the swell of her right breast, his breath hot against the bared skin revealed above the draped neckline of her gown.

Her cheeks warmed. 'I don't...'

'Are you, my angel?' He looked up at her, his gaze holding her captive.

'Just some black panties,' Andy felt compelled into acknowledging huskily.

'No bra. That's what I thought.' He continued to hold her gaze even as his head lowered and his lips encircled the fullness of her nipple over the material of her gown, his tongue a heated rasp as he licked across that highly sensitised tip.

Andy gasped as her back arched instinctively, succeeding in pushing her nipple deeper into the heat of Darius's mouth, at the same time as heated pleasure flooded her body. 'We should stop, Darius.' The protest sounded half-hearted even to Andy's own ears.

'I need to taste you!' he groaned achingly as he raised his head. 'How does this dress unfasten?'

'There's a catch on the shoulder, but...' Andy gave a shaky groan as Darius's fingers dealt far too swiftly with the fastening, allowing the material of her gown to cascade softly downwards, baring her completely to the waist.

Darius's gaze heated as he looked at her bared breasts, cupping each of them in his hands as the soft pads of his thumbs moved in a butterfly caress across the sensitive tips. Time and time again, until Andy groaned at each caress, her hands moving up to cling to the hardness of Darius's shoulders, as her knees threatened to buckle beneath her.

'Beautiful,' Darius murmured gruffly as he lowered his head, blowing gently on them before his lips parted to encircle one of those aroused nipples.

Andy's mesmerised gaze remained fixed on Darius, his lashes long and dark against the hardness of his cheeks as he laved her sensitive flesh with the moistness of his tongue, before suckling the nipple into the heat of his mouth, gently at first, and then more deeply, hungrily.

She could only groan her pleasure and watch in fascination as Darius's hand still cupped her other breast, his skin so much darker than her own, a finger and thumb lightly squeezing the other nipple to the same rhythm.

Watching Darius, lost in the sensations of his mouth and hands, was the most erotic experience of Andy's life.

She wanted more, needed more, as the pleasure grew and she moved restlessly against the hardness of Darius's thighs. Groaning low in her throat as he now rubbed his hardness into and against her, seeking and then finding the centre of her pleasure as he continued to thrust slowly against and into that aroused and swollen nubbin. Andy gasped as her body pulsed with hunger, needing, wanting to be filled.

Darius's mouth released her nipple with a soft pop before he straightened, his eyes a dark and enigmatic amber as he looked down at her, his cheeks flushed. 'Much as I would like to finish this here it's probably not a good idea.' He sighed his regret as he cupped both her breasts and bent to place a softly moist kiss on each swollen engorged tip before leaning back to reach for and refasten Andy's gown over her shoulder.

'Darius.'

'Duty first, pleasure later,' he promised huskily. 'Miranda?' he prompted sharply as she refused to meet his gaze.

Andy had never felt so mortified in her life. Or so out of control.

If Darius hadn't stopped when he had then Andy had no doubts she would have allowed him, no, *begged* him, to lay her across the conference table, like a sacrificial lamb, before making love to her. Her scars, be damned!

'Angel?' he pressed again gruffly.

Darius was studying her in frowning concentration when Andy finally forced herself to raise her head and look at him. To Darius this was nothing unusual, just another dalliance with a woman he desired to have in his bed for the night. Whereas for Andy it was—

For her it would have been the first time she had ever been so intimate with a man.

Not that she had deliberately or purposefully remained a virgin. There just hadn't been the time or opportunity during her years of hard work at ballet school. Or a man in her life since, that she cared enough about, for her to want to reveal her scars to.

And she very much doubted that Darius would want to take that sort of responsibility on himself, with any woman, let alone tutor a scarred—and scared!—virgin in how to make love.

Andy plastered a bright smile on her lips as she straightened. 'Of course.'

Darius forced himself not to say anything more as he unlocked the door and allowed Miranda to precede him out of the room before falling into step beside her, his hand light beneath her elbow, but his expression was grim as he tried to decide exactly what had just happened.

His main reason for taking Miranda out of the ballroom, and into the privacy of the small conference room, had been with the intention of allowing her the time to regain her composure after that encounter and conversation with Tia Bellamy. A meeting that had so obviously disturbed her.

He had kissed Miranda, again with the intention of distracting her.

Except he was now the one who was distracted.

He had enjoyed kissing Miranda.

Too much.

He had enjoyed making love with her.

Too much.

He had enjoyed caressing her and *tasting* her, and hearing her little breathy moans of pleasure.

All too damned much!

Her skin had felt so soft and silky beneath his questing lips. Her breasts were small but absolutely perfect. And her nipples, once he had unfastened the top of her gown and bared them to his heated gaze, were a delicious deep rose in colour, and so succulent to the taste as he suckled them deeply into his mouth, and lathed them with his tongue.

He had been so aroused, so lost in the enjoyment of her, Darius knew he could have gone on tasting her all night. Her breasts. Between her thighs. Every damn inch of her, from her head to her elegant toes.

So much so that he had almost made love to Miranda in a public conference room in one of his own hotels.

It was so far from his usual measured self-control that it was no wonder he now felt distracted.

'Hey, big bro!'

Darius blinked before a scowl settled between his eyes, and he focused on Xander with effort as his brother strolled down the hotel corridor towards them in the direction of the ballroom, obviously having finally decided to make an appearance at their mother's charity ball.

Darius's hand tightened instinctively on Miranda's elbow as he spoke to his brother. 'I should warn you, your tardiness has put you in Mother's bad books.'

Xander gave an unconcerned shrug as he grinned. 'She'll forgive me.' The darkness of his gaze turned interestedly towards Miranda as she stood silently at Darius's side.

It was an interest Darius was aware of taking exception to as he once again placed a proprietorial arm about Miranda's waist and anchored her to his side. Instantly causing Xander to eye him curiously.

'I have no doubts that Mother would forgive you if you admitted to having committed murder!' he dismissed dryly.

It was impossible for Andy not to compare the two brothers.

Darius was so dark and forbidding, Xander more a golden Viking god. An urbane and very handsome Viking god, to be sure, in his black dinner suit, his golden hair long enough to brush over the collar of his jacket.

It was because she had been watching the two of them so closely that Andy had seen the way in which Xander's eyes now darkened, the pupils almost obliterating the deep brown of the irises as his smile became fixed rather than humorous.

'Let's hope it never comes to that,' Xander

muttered as he avoided meeting his brother's gaze by turning his attention back to Andy, his expression instantly becoming flirtatious. 'An introduction would be nice, Darius?' he encouraged warmly.

'Miranda Jacobs, my brother Xander,' Darius bit out economically.

'Your *twin* brother,' Andy acknowledged lightly, deliberately stepping away from Darius's encircling arm about her waist as she shook hands with Xander.

Xander shot Darius an amused glance as he continued to hold her hand in his. 'Obviously I'm the handsome twin.'

'Oh, obviously!' She chuckled ruefully, finding Xander's flirtation and lazy charm much easier to deal with than the intensity of his brother's more mercurial moods.

Just as talking to Xander was also a welcome distraction from dwelling too much on thoughts of the heat of passion that had flared up so fiercely between herself and Darius just a short time ago.

'You can let go of her hand now, Xander.' Darius's voice was dark with his displeasure.

Because of his brother's flirtatious comment and the hold Xander had kept on Andy's hand?

She simply didn't know Darius well enough to be able to answer that question.

'Possessive, much?' His brother obviously felt no such uncertainty.

'Not in the least,' Darius dismissed harshly; he had never felt possessive over a woman in his life, least of all when it came to his own brother.

But then what explanation was there for his earlier sharpness towards Miranda, when he had thought she was far too interested in when or if Xander was going to be here too this evening?

As he was also far from pleased at watching Xander flirt with Miranda now?

Or the fact that he now wanted to slap Xander's hand away as it continued to hold Miranda's?

Whatever those feelings were, Darius wasn't comfortable with them. He didn't do possessive, any more than he did relationships.

He desired Miranda, wanted to make love to her, even more so after their lovemaking just now, but that was all this was. He had no doubts that once he'd had her in his bed his interest would wane, as it had with every other woman he had known.

'You really should go and make your apologies to Mother now,' Darius told his brother abruptly.

'Thank heavens for Charles, hmm?' Xander

grimaced. 'I do believe he could calm Mother down no matter what.'

'He loves her.' Darius nodded.

Xander's eyes glittered darkly. 'She deserves nothing less after being married to our bastard of a father for fourteen years.'

'Xander?' Darius was inwardly reeling even as he looked at his brother searchingly; none of them ever talked publicly—or privately either, come to that—of the brute of a man who had fathered the two of them and died when they were both thirteen. That Xander was doing so now, and in front of someone he had only just been introduced to, told Darius that something was very, *very* wrong with his brother.

Darius had been a little preoccupied, thinking of Miranda this past week, but he could see now that he should have been paying more attention to his twin. Xander had been playing hard the last few months, and he looked slightly pale tonight beneath the tan he had acquired in the Bahamas last month, and there was a reckless glitter in the dark depths of his eyes. Enough for Darius to be very concerned.

He gave a pained frown. 'Did you bring someone with you tonight, Xander?'

'I'm stag,' his brother dismissed as he glanced about them impatiently. 'Which means

I'm stuck with whatever woman Mother has decided it would be appropriate for me to sit beside at dinner!' His restlessness was barely contained.

'Maybe we could shift the seating around?'

'Don't bother on my account,' Xander bit out dismissively. 'I don't intend staying long, anyway. I'll look forward to seeing you again before I leave, though, Miranda,' he told her huskily, giving Darius one last rueful glance before striding off in the direction of the ballroom. And their mother.

Andy felt decidedly uncomfortable, once she and Darius were left alone together in the hallway, knowing by Darius's frown that he was disturbed by his brother's taciturn—and uncharacteristic?—behaviour.

From what Andy had read Xander was the relaxed, laid-back Sterne twin. The charmer. The playboy.

This evening Xander was anything but relaxed, the tension rolling off him in waves as he spoke of his mother's happy second marriage after her years of being married to their father.

Andy knew, from reading about Darius and Xander on the Internet, that Lomax Sterne had been the youngest son of a wealthy family, and that he had married Catherine Foster thirty-four years ago; their twin sons were born the following year. His death had been announced just thirteen years later, at the age of forty-two, after a fall down the stairs of the family's London home.

There had been no mention anywhere of any dissension in the marriage.

It was obvious to Andy, from the frown still creasing Darius's brow, that he was more than a little worried about his twin. 'Look, something has obviously upset your brother, and I really don't mind if you need to go and talk to him. I can easily get a taxi home.'

'No,' Darius bit out grimly as he straightened to look down at her through narrowed lids.

The truth was that Andy would have welcomed the excuse to leave; Darius's concern for Xander apart, she had no idea how she was expected to spend the rest of the evening with Darius after the intimacies they had just shared. After she had allowed herself to be seduced by Darius's kisses, and the pleasurable caress of his mouth and hands on her bared breasts.

'Ready?' Darius asked as he held out his arm for her to take.

The answer to that was a definite no!

Andy had a feeling she would never be ready for a man like Darius.

He really was just too much. Of everything. And Andy was far too inexperienced to even begin to know how to deal with a man like him.

So much so that all she wanted to do was make her excuses and flee into the night, back to the safety of her apartment and dance studio.

Instead she drew in a deep breath before answering him. 'If you're sure?'

Darius nodded tersely. 'I'm very sure.'

Andy kept her lashes lowered as she placed her hand in the crook of Darius's arm and allowed him to accompany her back into the ballroom.

All the time she was aware of the way the silky material of her gown moved caressingly across her sensitised nipples, a stark reminder that Darius had suckled and stroked them so pleasurably just minutes ago.

'That wasn't so bad, was it?' Darius turned in his seat to look at Miranda once the tables, arranged about the dance floor for dinner, had been cleared at the end of the meal in readiness for the dancing to come later.

Most of the other guests had now left their

tables in order to go and freshen up, or circulate and talk to other guests, while the orchestra prepared for the next part of the evening.

'The food was very good,' Miranda answered him stiltedly.

'The food but not the company, hmm?' He gave a grimace. 'Once again my ego is shot down in flames!'

Andy felt the warmth of colour in her cheeks. 'I didn't mean to imply...'

'Of course you did.' Darius chuckled. 'Admit it, Miranda, you *enjoy* shooting me down in flames.'

She did, yes. But only in an effort to hide the desire she knew she felt for him. Although after her undeniable response to Darius earlier, that was probably a complete waste of her time.

She still felt utterly mortified every time she so much as thought of those earlier intimacies. It had been absolute agony to sit beside him during dinner and pretend that she was relaxed, and everything was okay between the two of them; her senses were now so heightened towards Darius that she was totally aware of his every move.

For his part, Darius had seemed completely unaffected, by her or his earlier concern for his brother. He'd been totally at his ease as he'd introduced her to the other guests seated at their table, all of whom he appeared to know. He had also made a point of including her in the conversation, and he had been nothing but polite and attentive to her needs during the meal.

No, obviously Andy was the only one who was still totally unnerved by earlier.

As she had been unsettled, after glancing about the room earlier, to see that Xander had been seated next to Tia, of all people. As evidence, no doubt, that Catherine Latimer knew Tia was one of the country's prima ballerinas, even if one of her sons, at least, didn't.

The look of triumph Tia had shot in Andy's direction didn't bode well either. Not that there was anything Andy could do about that.

No, the reason for the return of her tension now could only be attributed to one thing: the orchestra was tuning up ready to start playing so that the dancing part of the evening could begin. Dancing that Andy had no intention of being a part of.

She straightened in her seat. 'I think I'd like to leave now. I'm feeling rather tired, and no doubt, despite what you said earlier, you would like the opportunity to go and talk to your brother?'

Darius wasn't fooled for a moment by Miranda's excuse of tiredness, knew only too well that her intention was to avoid the possibility of his asking her to dance. Not only in public, this time, but in front of one of her ex-associates.

Miranda might have refused to satisfy his curiosity in that regard earlier, but Darius *knew* there was something else between Miranda and Tia Bellamy. And, before too much time had passed, he intended to discover exactly what that was.

His mouth firmed. 'Xander isn't in the mood to talk right now. And we aren't leaving until after I've danced with you again.'

'No.'

'Yes.'

Her face paled at his insistence. 'You can't make me dance with you, Darius.'

He arched one dark eyebrow. 'No?'

She glared. 'No!'

'Your always questionable charm doesn't appear to be working right now, Darius,' Xander taunted as he came to stand beside the table where the two of them sat quietly arguing. 'Let's see if I have any more luck.'

He turned to look down at Miranda with warm and teasing brown eyes, his bad mood of earlier seeming to have dissipated.

'Would you do me the honour of dancing

the first dance with me, Miranda?' he invited huskily as the orchestra began to play and the elegantly dressed couples immediately began to take to the dance floor.

A part of Andy so wanted to say yes to Xander's invitation, if only as a way of putting Darius and his damned arrogance firmly in their place.

But common sense warned her against doing that. For two reasons.

Firstly, she really didn't want to dance, with either of the Sterne brothers.

Secondly, the challenging glitter in Darius's eyes told her that she would undoubtedly pay a price if she were to accept and dance with Xander after having refused him.

A price, after her responses to Darius earlier, Andy was afraid she might be only too willing to pay, and damn the consequences!

She smiled up at Xander politely. 'I would rather not, but thank you for asking.'

'So much for your own charm being more effective than mine!' Darius eyed his brother mockingly.

'Hey, it was worth a try.' Xander seemed unconcerned as he pulled out the empty chair on Andy's other side before sitting down. 'I have no idea who that woman was sitting next to me at dinner, and it took me a few minutes to realise she was actually talking about you, Miranda, because she kept referring to you as Andy.'

'Only your brother insists on calling me by my full name,' Andy explained wryly.

'Interesting,' Xander murmured slowly as he gave Darius a speculative glance. 'Anyway, the woman has it in for you, Miranda.' He eyed her shrewdly.

A shrewdness that alerted Andy to the fact that, despite what the media might report to the contrary, Xander Sterne was every bit as hard-edged and astute as his twin brother. He just chose to hide it better than the more arrogantly forthright Darius.

She gave a shrug. 'Tia and I once worked together.'

Xander huffed. 'Not harmoniously, I'm guessing.'

Andy gave a small smile. 'It was a long time ago.'

He shrugged. 'That doesn't seem to have tempered her dislike any.'

Andy was more than a little curious to know exactly what Tia had said about her to Xander Sterne to have alerted him to that fact. But it was a curiosity she had no intention of satisfying when Darius was listening to the conversation so intently. He had already shown he was more than a little curious about her past relationship with Tia.

'It was just a little healthy rivalry, that's all.'

'It didn't seem all that healthy to me,' Xander warned as he looked across at his brother. 'I should keep an eye out for knives in Miranda's back, if I were you, Darius. The woman tries to hide it, but she's obviously got a problem with Miranda.'

'I already gathered that after we spoke to her earlier,' Darius drawled. 'And the only thing that is going to be anywhere near Miranda's back in the near future, or her front either, for that matter, is me!' he added with a challenging glance at Andy.

'Darius.' Andy gasped, even as her face blushed a fiery red. 'That was totally uncalled for,' she added with an uncomfortable glance at the now grinning Xander.

'But true,' Darius replied with infuriating confidence.

'Have you two known each other long?' Xander relaxed back in his chair as he watched them with amusement.

'Too long!'

'A few days.'

Andy and Darius both spoke at the same time, Andy irritably, Darius with as much amusement as his brother.

'It might seem longer, Miranda, but it really is only a few days,' Darius added dryly.

'Well, you know the answer to that: don't ask me out again!' she countered tartly, causing Xander to chuckle appreciatively.

'Oh, I wasn't complaining, Miranda.' Darius sat forward to place his hand over one of hers, his fingers curling tightly about hers as he felt her attempt to pull away. 'Quite the opposite, in fact,' he added huskily, his gaze holding hers captive as his hand continued to hold onto her slender fingers.

'I'm starting to feel like a definite third wheel here,' Xander murmured speculatively.

Darius shot his brother a narrow-eyed glance. 'Then I suggest you go and find your own woman and stop trying to flirt with mine.'

He ignored Miranda's outraged gasp this time as he glanced across Xander's shoulder. 'What the hell…?' He gave an impatient shake of his head. 'What is this? A family convention? Mother is on her way over here too now,' he huffed.

'Definitely my cue to leave.' Xander stood up abruptly.

'I'm guessing your charm didn't work there earlier, either?' Darius drawled.

'Not enough for me to be willing to stay around and listen to more scolding about my tardiness.' Xander grimaced. 'It was really good to meet you, Miranda,' he added warmly.

'You too,' she barely had time to murmur, before Xander had turned and disappeared onto the crowded dance floor.

Darius released Miranda's hand, standing up politely as his mother reached their table. 'What a shame—you just missed Xander,' he said.

His mother frowned. 'It wasn't Xander I wanted to talk to.'

'No? Well, unfortunately Miranda and I were just leaving.'

Andy shot him a sharp glance. Deservedly so, when just minutes ago Darius had insisted they weren't leaving until she had danced with him again. Obviously the arrival of his mother had succeeded in changing his plans where Andy's refusal hadn't.

'I really must apologise for not recognising you earlier, Miss Jacobs.' Catherine Latimer turned to her, her tone warmly charming. 'I knew you looked familiar, but Charles was the one who realised who you are, and I simply had to come and tell you how much I enjoyed watching you dance in *Giselle* four…or was it five years ago?'

Darius saw all the colour leech from Miranda's cheeks before she answered his mother woodenly. 'It was four and a half years ago.'

'Of course it was.' His mother beamed. 'Such a wonderful talent. So much promise. Such a tragedy about your accident—'

'Mother—'

'But you are obviously fully recovered from that now.' Catherine beamed, completely undaunted by Darius's attempt to silence her. 'I'm organising a charity gala performance for next month, and I appreciate that it's short notice, but I was wondering if you would be willing to give a ten-minute performance? Possibly something from *Swan Lake*?'

'Mother!'

'Darius, do stop interrupting when I'm talking to Ms Jacobs.'

His mother shot him an irritated glance before turning back to smile at Miranda. 'I can't tell you what a thrill it would be for everyone if you would agree to perform.'

'That is quite enough, Mother!' Darius thundered as Miranda seemed to go even paler, her eyes huge green wells of despair against that pallor. 'More than enough,' he added grimly. 'Miranda will not be dancing at one of your charity galas, next month or at any other time.'

He pulled Miranda effortlessly to her feet

to stand beside him, his arm moving about her waist and securing her at his side as she seemed to sway slightly.

'You're being very high-handed, Darius.' Catherine frowned her disapproval. 'I'm sure that Ms Jacobs is more than capable of answering for herself.'

Not at the moment she wasn't. In fact, Darius felt sure that if he didn't get Miranda out of here in the next few minutes she was going to do one of two things. One, be extremely rude to his mother, which Darius had no doubt she would later regret, Or two, she might just faint, which she would also later regret. The last thing Miranda would want was to draw attention to herself. To perhaps be recognised by more people than his mother and stepfather and Tia Bellamy.

Miranda definitely would not want to cause a scene in front of Tia Bellamy.

His mouth tightened. 'As I said, Miranda and I were just leaving, Mother.'

'But...'

Darius's glare finally seemed to have penetrated his mother's dogged determination as she fell suddenly silent. 'I'll call you tomorrow, Mother,' he promised tightly, not waiting for her to answer this time as he guided

Miranda effortlessly through and away from the crowded and noisy ballroom.

Aware as he did so of the shocked expression on her deathly white face and the trembling of her slender body beside his own.

As aware as Darius was that he was the one who had insisted—blackmailed her—into stepping into this vipers' den this evening.

CHAPTER SIX

Darius collected Miranda's wrap from the cloakroom and got the two of them out of the hotel in the minimum of time and with the minimum of effort, making sure the still silent Miranda was comfortably seated in the passenger seat of his car the moment it was brought round to the front entrance of the hotel, before quietly thanking the valet and climbing in behind the wheel of the vehicle and pulling away.

The two of them drove along the busy London streets in silence for some minutes, Miranda obviously still slightly shell-shocked from the conversation with his mother. Darius brooded over the fact that he was responsible for having placed Miranda in that vulnerable position in the first place. Not once but twice.

First with Tia Bellamy.

And then again with his mother.

What the hell had his mother been thinking

of, just coming over to Miranda in that way and bluntly asking her to perform for her?

No, damn it, his mother wasn't to blame for any of what had happened tonight; *he* was. Miranda hadn't wanted to go to the charity dinner with him in the first place; Darius had blackmailed her into attending. And his mother's conversation hadn't been the start of the disintegration of the evening, either—that encounter with Tia Bellamy had.

'I'm sorry.'

Andy was so lost in thought that for a moment she wasn't even aware that Darius had spoken. Her eyes widened in surprise when his words finally registered. Was the arrogant Darius Sterne actually apologising to her? And if so, exactly what was he apologising for?

Although she couldn't deny, one way or another, the evening *had* been something of a disaster.

Attending the charity dinner at all had been an ordeal forced upon her by Darius himself.

Being introduced to Darius's parents had been nerve-racking.

Meeting Tia Bellamy again had been even worse.

The time alone with Darius in that conference room still made Andy blush just to think of it.

The conversation with Xander before dinner had also been a little strange, revealing a more brooding and complex man than any of the press had ever reported seeing.

Catherine Latimer coming over to them just now, and asking Andy if she would consider dancing at the gala concert she was organising for next month, had been a total shock.

But it had been intriguing too, if Andy was being completely honest.

There was no way she would be able to dance professionally ever again; her hip and thigh, although strong enough for everyday activity and a minimum of dancing at her studio, just weren't capable of taking the rigorous physical demands of a full-time career in ballet. But that didn't mean Andy couldn't still dance, it just meant the amount of time she could perform, at any one time, was limited. A five-or ten-minute performance, on behalf of charity, was not only possible but also tempting. Very tempting.

Hence Andy's distraction now.

Was she seriously considering Catherine Latimer's invitation?

And she still had no idea precisely what Darius was now apologising for when so much of the evening had been fraught with tension.

To such a degree that Andy now felt hysterical laughter welling up from deep within her. Really, could the evening have been any *more* of a disaster?

Maybe if Kim had been there too, glowering her disapproval of Darius Sterne on top of everything else that had gone wrong with the evening.

It had been one trauma after another from start to finish. Andy certainly doubted that roller coaster of emotion was what Darius usually expected when he deigned to take a woman out for the evening. It was—

Well, it was hilarious—that was what it was, Andy acknowledged, and she gave an inelegant snort as she tried to resist the laughter that threatened to burst free. And failed.

'Miranda?' Darius shot Miranda an anxious glance as he heard her draw in a deep breath and then give a choked sob. 'Oh, hell, Miranda, please don't cry!' he groaned, frantically looking for a side road he could turn the car into so that he could park up and take Miranda into his arms.

Miranda's only answer was to bury her face in her hands, her shoulders shaking as she obviously began to cry in earnest.

'Hell!' Darius muttered again darkly, no longer waiting for the right opportunity to get out of the traffic but just flicking on the indicator to signal he was turning the car off the main road.

He lifted his hand in apology to a couple of other drivers as they tooted their protest as he eased the Bentley in front of their vehicles and down into a narrow side road; consideration for other drivers wasn't high on his list of priorities at the moment—Miranda was.

He pulled the car in next to the pavement and parked before switching off the engine and turning to reach across the leather divide to take Miranda into his arms. 'I really am sorry I put you through any of this evening, Miranda,' he murmured into the perfumed silkiness of her hair as she now shook in his arms.

Her only answer was to draw in another sharp breath followed by another sob, as she continued to keep her face buried in her hands and her shoulders shook even harder.

Darius wasn't sure how to deal with a woman's tears. Well, he wasn't sure how to deal with Miranda's tears.

He was more used to the beautiful women he dated using pouting and wheedling in order to get their own way. And he had certainly grown immune, over the years, to his mother's brand of emotional manipulation.

But Miranda wasn't like any of those

women. She was too forthright to use whee-dling, and she definitely wasn't the type of woman to emotionally manipulate a man.

If she had been Darius might not have felt quite so impotent right now.

'Miranda…'

He paused, Miranda having finally low-ered her hands from her face before lifting her head to look up at him, and frowned his confusion as he saw that Miranda wasn't cry-ing but laughing. Well…her cheeks were cer-tainly wet with tears, but they appeared to be tears of laughter rather than distress.

'Miranda?' Darius eyed her uncertainly.

She gave a shake of her head. 'Wasn't that just the most awful night of your life?' She chuckled, green eyes gleaming with that same humour. 'All it needed to make it horrendously perfect was the disapproving presence of my older sister.'

Darius released her to slowly lean back in his own seat, his expression perplexed as he studied her through narrowed lids across the dimmed interior of the car.

In his experience, most women would have taken full advantage right now of the fact that he was responsible for blackmailing her into the midst of that sequence of awkward situa-tions, and they would have made sure he paid a price for it too, either in the form of an expensive gift, or some other form of manipulation. Not Miranda. Miranda was *laughing*.

It was the first time Darius had seen her laugh without restraint. The green of her eyes gleamed with amusement; it brought a flush to her cheeks; her lips curved into the fullness of a relaxed smile. She looked younger and more carefree than he had ever seen her. And incredibly beautiful.

Although Darius wasn't a hundred per cent sure it was altogether flattering, hearing her class the time the two of them had spent together in the conference room as part of the most awful night of her life.

'Oh, come on, Darius,' Andy encouraged as she saw the frown between his eyes. 'Admit it, it was so awful there's nothing else to do but laugh.' She took a tissue from her clutch bag and mopped the dampness from her cheeks.

'It had its moments of humour,' he allowed grudgingly.

Andy grinned across at him. 'It had all of the hallmarks of a disaster movie.'

He eyed her irritably. 'I don't consider all of the evening to have been a disaster.'

Andy pretended to give the idea some thought, hoping that in the dimly lit interior of the car Darius couldn't see the blush in her cheeks that revealed that she knew exactly which part of the evening he was referring to. 'Well, no,' she finally conceded. 'For instance, I very much enjoyed finally meeting your brother.'

Darius scowled. 'I'm not sure I didn't prefer you *before* you discovered your sense of humour.'

The past four years had been a bit grim, Andy acknowledged ruefully, so maybe she had lost her sense of humour along the way too?

If that was the case she had certainly rediscovered it this evening. Necessarily so. It was either laugh or curl up in a ball and feel sorry for herself, and she had no intentions of doing that; her days of self-pity had been over long ago.

'Oh, that remark had nothing to do with humour, Darius; Xander is extremely handsome, and he was very charming after dinner.'

'As opposed to…?'

'Xander is extremely handsome and charming,' she repeated dryly.

He scowled. 'Xander was far from in a charming mood when he arrived at the hotel this evening.'

'Something had obviously upset him, but he got over it.'

'Meaning?'

Andy shrugged. 'The mood was unusual rather than the norm.'

'Unlike some people you could mention?'

She gave him an innocent glance. 'I repeat, I found him extremely handsome and charming.'

Darius felt his lips twitch as he tried to control the smile threatening and failed utterly. 'You really are determined to shatter my ego.' He chuckled.

'I believe a little humility to be a great leveller,' she added pertly.

Darius felt his admiration and liking for this woman grow. Miranda was only twenty-three, and she had already been through so much. She had lost both her parents at only eighteen, and then suffered through the worst disappointment of her life, when her career in ballet came to such a tragic and abrupt end just months later.

But Miranda had survived. She was a survivor, carving out another career for herself, and now he also learnt that she could laugh at herself, and him, even in the midst of the type of adversity she had suffered through this evening.

'Have lunch with me tomorrow?' he asked

without giving himself time to consider the wisdom of the invitation.

He had no doubts that Miranda was slowly but surely burrowing not just beneath his natural reserve, but also past the barrier he had kept about his emotions for so many years. Tonight he had realised that he not only felt desire for Miranda, but also protectiveness. He didn't want to see Miranda hurt by the actions of others, like Tia Bellamy who'd slighted her deliberately, his mother less so, but she had still upset her nonetheless. And Darius hadn't liked seeing Miranda unhappy. At all.

The smile slowly fading from her lips and the warmth from her eyes, she looked across at him searchingly, the interior of the car illuminated from the street lamp outside. 'Why?' she finally enquired warily.

There was no hesitation in Darius's laughter this time as he chuckled throatily. 'Maybe I would just like to take you out to lunch.'

'But it's Sunday.'

'And?'

She shrugged. 'Sunday is a day to spend with family, eating roast lunch, before lounging around watching an old movie together on TV in the afternoon, stuff like that.'

'Is that what you're doing tomorrow?'

'Well, no,' she answered slowly. 'But that's only because it's Kim and Colin's turn to spend the day with Colin's parents.'

Darius nodded. 'It all sounds idyllic, but to my knowledge my own mother has never cooked a Sunday roast for her family in her life, nor have we ever all lounged around watching an old movie on the television together on a Sunday afternoon.'

Before her parents died, and when her school and ballet schedule had allowed, Andy had always gone home on a Sunday to spend time with her family. And when she had it had usually involved helping her mother to cook the family meal, before they all overate and then watched a really old film on the television together.

Darius was a billionaire, could buy whatever he wanted, no doubt employed a housekeeper or cook to take care of him—or both!—and he could also eat in the most expensive restaurants all over the world, but he had never enjoyed anything so simple as a Sunday lunch cooked and eaten at home with his family, before spending the day together?

'I really don't want to go out to lunch, but if you would care to come round to my apartment at about twelve-thirty tomorrow, then you'll be in time to join me for lunch.

No blackmail involved in the invitation,' she added dryly.

And then berated herself for having made the invitation at all. Okay, so this evening had been awful enough to be considered funny, but there was no escaping the fact that Darius had also kissed and touched and caressed her, more intimately than any other man had ever done.

Or that by inviting him to her apartment tomorrow, for *any* reason, she was simply asking for a repeat of the same. Literally *inviting* a repeat of the same.

'Your brother-in-law's job is safe, Miranda,' Darius answered her abruptly. 'Turns out he's the best IT guy Midas Enterprises employs anywhere.'

She eyed him derisively. 'The invitation to Sunday lunch still stands.'

Darius looked irritated. 'You aren't my mother, Miranda!'

Her eyes widened at the ludicrousness of that statement, given the circumstances. 'I think we're both only too well aware of that,' she answered tartly.

'And I assure you, I don't feel in the least deprived because my mother has never cooked me a roast meal for Sunday lunch.'

Of course he didn't. He was Darius Sterne,

billionaire businessman and successful entre-
preneur. A man who owned homes in several
capital cities around the world. A man who
owned his own private jet. The same man who
had paid thousands of pounds for two tickets so that they could attend a charity dinner
this evening. What had Andy been thinking
of, inviting him to her apartment, for a home-
cooked Sunday lunch?

She sighed. 'Fine, I was only being polite
anyway, by returning your own invitation.'

'But without the blackmail,' he reminded
her dryly.

'Just forget I asked.'

'Now I've offended you.'

'I don't offend that easily.'

'Lunch at your apartment sounds…'

'Boring. Mundane.' She nodded. 'As I said,
just forget I asked.'

'No, actually it sounds…' Darius paused
with a frown, uncertain how to proceed.

Going to Miranda's apartment, eating a
lunch that she had cooked and prepared, actually sounded rather nice. And very intimate.
In a way that Darius usually avoided where
women were concerned. Not that any of the
models or society heiresses he had briefly
dated in the past had ever suggested cooking
a meal for him, but even so.

'It sounds good. Thank you,' he added abruptly. 'I'll bring the wine, shall I?'

Andy eyed him ruefully, seriously wondering if Darius had ever eaten a meal cooked in a woman's apartment by her, for him, let alone made the polite offer to bring the wine to accompany that meal.

And, no, she accepted that couldn't be described as deprived, exactly, but it was more normal behaviour, surely, than eating meals either cooked by your own personal cook or housekeeper, or out in exclusive restaurants or hotels?

Maybe being a billionaire had its drawbacks, after all?

Oh, she didn't doubt that it must be wonderful not to have any money worries, ever, but what about missing out on some of the simple things in life? Such as family meals and time together? Walks in the bluebell woods? Or just sitting in companionable silence with someone reading a book? Surely all that money put Darius above enjoying such everyday things?

Or maybe it was just a case of what you'd never had you'd never think to miss? In the same way that Andy had never had money, so didn't miss it, Darius had been born into a wealthy family, old money, and he and his brother had only increased that wealth a thousandfold, and so ensuring that he never lived any other way.

In which case, lunch in her rustic and open loft apartment was going to be a novel experience for him.

'A bottle of red will be great,' she accepted, having just decided that she would cook roast beef with all the trimmings; if she was going to do this, then she might as well do it properly. 'And it's informal,' she added firmly.

So far in their acquaintance she had only ever seen Darius in formal clothes, such as tailored suits, or the tailored dinner suit he was wearing this evening. How good would he look in a pair of well-worn figure-hugging jeans, resting low down on the leanness of his hips, and a tight T-shirt moulded to his muscular shoulders and chest, the darkness of his overlong hair sexily tousled onto his brow?

Just the thought of it was enough to cause her to quiver in anticipation.

And those sorts of thoughts were going to get her into even more trouble where this man was concerned. More than she already was? Oh, yes.

She straightened in her seat. 'Could we head back to my apartment now? It's been a long and eventful evening.'

Darius continued to study Miranda's face

for several long seconds, noting the attractive flush to her cheeks, the brightness of those green eyes, the pouting fullness of her lips. He wanted nothing more than to kiss that fullness again, to taste Miranda, to touch her, as he had kissed and touched her earlier.

It took every effort of will on his part to instead settle back in his seat and turn the car key in the ignition. He deliberately didn't look at Miranda again as they drove the rest of the way to her apartment in silence.

Still, he was completely aware of everything about her. Of the warmth of her body, so close to his own in the confines of the car. Of the perfume he was learning to associate with Miranda, something floral and slightly exotic. The way the silence between them now felt companionable rather than uncomfortable.

Intimate.

There was that word again.

And this thing between himself and Miranda, whatever it was, was definitely becoming too intimate for comfort.

His comfort.

It was a physical discomfort, at least, that returned the moment Darius arrived at Miranda's apartment the following day, and she opened the door to him wearing skinny jeans, and an over-large green T-shirt that revealed the tantalising outline of her breasts. She'd tied her ash-blonde hair in a ponytail, and her face was completely bare of make-up. Her feet were bare too.

Her completely natural and unaffected beauty left him momentarily speechless.

The last thing Darius had wanted, after he had spent a restless night unable to sleep, and then most of the morning considering picking up the telephone and calling Miranda to cancel their lunch. The only thing that had stopped him from making that call was that he had a feeling Miranda would have seen his excuse for exactly what it was: a deliberate effort on his part to distance himself from her.

Because she was getting too close.

Dangerously so.

And he wanted her to be even closer.

He wanted Miranda close enough that he knew everything there was to know about her. What her favourite food was. Her favourite colour. Her taste in films and books. Who her friends were. What her ambitions were for her dance studio. What else she wanted for her future.

What she looked for in a lover. He especially wanted to discover that.

As he wanted Miranda to know those same

things about him. Funny, he had never before wanted any of those things with any woman.

But one look at Miranda now and he felt sure he should have listened to his head and cancelled this lunch.

She tilted her head and eyed him quizzically as she opened the door wider, her ponytail falling across one shoulder. 'It isn't too late to change your mind.'

Darius gave her an irritated scowl; were his mood and thoughts really so readable to this woman? Probably—he'd never been good at concealing his emotions, which was why he tried his best to avoid engaging them in the first place.

'Darius?' she asked. 'Are you coming in or would you rather just continue to stand out there on the stairs? You may find it uncomfortable to eat your lunch, but it's your choice.'

It wasn't only the challenge she presented, or the mouth-watering smell of lunch cooking coming from inside the apartment, that caused Darius to abruptly hand her the bottle of wine as he stepped inside, but also the curiosity he felt to see Miranda's space. She'd insisted he left her at the door last night and now he wanted to see for himself what type of home she had made for herself.

The interior was a complete open loft space

the same floor size as the ballet school below, the walls were of exposed brickwork and dark wooden beams bisected the ceiling above. The space itself was divided into zones, with a rustic kitchen in one corner, a table and chairs already set for eating on the other side of the island unit. The sofa and chairs beside the fireplace were comfortable rather than modern, and the floor was covered in colourful rugs. The colours were all earth tones: terracotta, yellows, greens, with touches of russet.

There were several Degas ballet prints hanging on the exposed brickwork, with that open fireplace at one end of the massive room, and half a dozen steps led up to a smaller mezzanine level, which, Darius presumed, encompassed the sleeping area and bathroom.

It was the complete opposite to the ultramodern apartments he owned, in several capitals of the world, including London. His places had all been furnished and decorated by fashionably exclusive interior designers.

In contrast to their cool sterility, Miranda's apartment was warmly comfortable, and extremely welcoming.

It was just the sort of space, a place of calm and tranquillity, where it would be possible to totally relax, away from the rush and bustle of the world beyond these four walls.

Andy had absolutely no idea what thoughts were going through Darius's mind as he looked about her apartment, his expression non-committal.

She only hoped that her own expression was just as unreadable to him!

Her fantasy of a dressed-down Darius didn't do justice to the man now standing before her. His faded jeans showed off the perfection of his taut backside and the long lean length of his legs. A black short-sleeved T-shirt revealed the muscled length of his arms, and stretched over wide shoulders, muscled chest and flat stomach. The darkness of his overlong hair was deliciously tousled, as if he might have showered and washed it just before leaving home, leaving it to dry naturally on the drive over here.

He looked completely male and completely gorgeous.

Breathtakingly so.

Knee-tremblingly so.

Andy had spent several hours debating what she should wear today, almost every item of clothing she possessed having ended up discarded on the bed as she vetoed one outfit after another. She had finally settled on her usual Sunday clothes, of comfortable jeans and an over-large T-shirt, hoping the familiarity would help her to get through the next few hours in Darius's company.

Although, from the way Darius had looked at her when he'd arrived, she had been wasting her time, and comfort was the last thing he saw when he looked at her.

'Would you like to open the bottle of wine and let it breathe for a few minutes while I put the finishing touches to lunch?' Andy's gaze was lowered as she placed the bottle and opener on top of the breakfast bar before turning her back as she diligently stirred the gravy in a saucepan on top of the hob.

This had been a bad idea, she chastised herself for what had to be the hundredth time since making the invitation the previous evening. She was totally aware of Darius standing a short distance away as he, no doubt deftly, took the cork from the bottle of wine.

She had gone out shopping for food as soon as the shops had opened this morning, half hoping Darius would have left a message on the answer-machine when she got back, cancelling joining her for lunch. No such luck, and when it had reached midday, with still no word from him, Andy had decided to accept the inevitable: she would have to get through several hours of having Darius in her apartment today, while the two of them ate lunch together.

But that was all they were going to do. There would be no lounging around together afterwards, no sitting cosily on the sofa and watching a film on the television, or any of that other relaxing—but with Darius, dangerous —Sunday stuff.

'This is nice.'

Andy's hand shook slightly as she stirred the gravy, with Darius standing so close to her the warmth of his breath brushed against the back of her neck. 'It's home,' she dismissed without turning.

'I wasn't referring to your apartment,' he said softly.

Oh, heavens.

This really had been a bad idea.

Probably the worst idea she had ever had in her life.

Andy drew in a sharp breath before turning to face him, her heart pounding in her chest as she looked up and found herself instantly captivated by his eyes. As the cologne he wore—that smell of lemons with an underlying spice—wound itself insidiously about her senses.

She swallowed before speaking, so aware that time seemed to have stopped. One of them had to break the tension of the moment. 'Would you like to carve the beef at the table or shall I do it now and put it on the plates?' She tried to sound normal, but her voice sounded unusually husky in the tense silence wrapping itself tightly about the two of them.

Darius watched Miranda's mouth as she spoke, once again mesmerised by the fullness of her lips. They were beautifully curved, completely bare of lip gloss, and he ached to kiss them until they were a full and swollen pout.

Next he wanted to remove her T-shirt and bra and taste her breasts again…

Before unfastening and then peeling her figure-hugging jeans down the long length of her legs. Then he longed to remove her panties so that he could kiss and taste the lushness between her thighs. More than anything else he wanted to finish what they had started the evening before, to kiss Miranda, caress and stroke her with his hands, lips and tongue, and refuse to release her until she cried out her pleasure.

None of which fell in with the plan Darius had had when he'd arrived, which was to eat lunch, thank Miranda very politely, before getting the hell out of here.

What *was* it about this woman, in particular, that totally robbed him of the reserve and control that had never once been shaken before?

She wasn't even his type, and she was definitely too innocent and inexperienced for him. Miranda would probably run away screaming if she knew some of the things he had imagined doing to and with her as he lay awake in bed last night, unable to sleep!

'Darius?'

He gave a slightly dazed shake of his head as he stepped abruptly back and away from her. 'I'm fine leaving you to carve the meat.'

Andy gave a shrug as Darius turned and walked away; her father had always carved the meat at the table, and Colin now carried on that tradition, but it was probably a little too domesticated for the sophisticated billionaire Darius Sterne.

Probably?

This man was about as domesticated as a jungle cat—and just as lethal!

He moved like one too, Andy noted a little breathlessly as she once again found herself unable to stop watching Darius as he crossed the room with stealthy grace before studying the prints on her walls, the muscles moving tautly in his back and the delicious outline of his hard and muscled backside, outlined so perfectly in those fitted jeans.

'Everything okay?' He turned to look at her, eyebrows raised questioningly.

Andy gave a start as she realised she was still staring at Darius's edible backside rather than serving the lunch, as she'd said she was going to do.

'Fine.' She nodded abruptly before forcing herself to turn away from that probing gaze and instead busying herself carving the meat and placing the food into the serving dishes.

The sooner Darius ate then, hopefully, the sooner he would leave again.

CHAPTER SEVEN

'NOT ONLY BEAUTIFUL, but you also know how to cook!' Darius looked appreciatively across the table at Miranda once they had finished what had turned out to be a very enjoyable meal.

And not just because the food had been every bit as good as it smelt.

No, once they had got over that initial tension, and had begun to eat their meal, the conversation had actually flowed quite naturally between them, and whether Miranda realised it or not Darius now knew the answer to at least some of the things he had been curious about earlier. Miranda's favourite colour was red, her favourite food Italian, and she liked to read murder mysteries. And as that was Darius's preference too, they had then had quite a lively discussion on the merits of certain authors as opposed to others.

'A multi-tasker—that's me,' Miranda lightly brushed off the compliment as she stood up with the obvious intention of clearing away the dishes.

Darius put a restraining hand on the bareness of her arm. 'Sit and finish your wine, and I'll tidy these things away,' he instructed as he stood up.

'Helpful as well as handsome?' she came back dryly.

Darius gave a slow smile. 'Well, I'll settle for handsome certainly.'

Miranda frowned as she obviously realised her teasing had backfired on her. 'Don't you usually have an army of minions to do this sort of thing for you?' she teased as she slowly sat down and watched him clear the table.

'Now, now, Miranda, let's not spoil the day by arguing again,' Darius drawled, before slowly stilling as he looked down at her through narrowed lids. 'Or maybe that was your intention?'

Was that what Andy was trying to do? Put the distance back between them, by deliberately challenging him?

Maybe she was being contentious. Because she was feeling so defensive, after the last few hours had passed more pleasurably than she could ever have imagined. Darius had relaxed in a way Andy hadn't believed he ever could, as they'd discussed books and theatre and art as they ate. No doubt the delicious red wine had also contributed to their becoming so relaxed in each other's company.

But it wasn't real, Andy reminded herself firmly.

Darius was…who he was. And she was who she was.

Outside this apartment, this moment in time, their lives were totally different.

Too different for them to have any reason to see each other again after today.

Even if Darius suggested it. Which Andy had no reason to suppose that he would.

'Obviously it was.' Darius sighed his frustration with her silence. 'What have I done to make you distrust me so much—other than using blackmail to get you to go to the charity dinner with me?' He grimaced.

'Isn't that enough?' Andy gazed up at him crossly. 'Darius, normal people don't use blackmail to force someone into going out with them!' she added as he looked down at her questioningly.

His mouth thinned. 'You were being intransigent.'

She gasped. 'And that gives you the right to use my brother-in-law's job to blackmail me?'

A nerve pulsed in his tightly clenched jaw.

'It gives me the right to use whatever means are necessary.'

'No, Darius.' Andy gave a slow shake of her head. 'It really doesn't.'

Darius eyed her impatiently. Obviously, whatever truce had existed between them while they ate was now over. 'Why don't you go and see if there's a film on television we can watch together, while I clear away here?'

Miranda's eyes widened. 'You're staying?'

It hadn't been his original intention, no. The opposite, in fact. But somehow, this past couple of hours with Miranda had been more enjoyable, more real to him, than anything else had felt for a very long time. And Darius wasn't willing to give that up just yet.

He shrugged. 'I thought watching a film was part of the Sunday family ritual.'

She blinked. 'You aren't family.'

Darius gave an unconcerned grin. 'We could always pretend that I am.'

'No,' she drawled. 'We really couldn't.'

He quirked a brow. 'No?'

Andy's eyes narrowed; anyone less like a member of her very normal family she simply couldn't imagine. She was also a little thrown that Darius now intended staying on after lunch; she had felt sure that he wouldn't want to, that a couple of hours of normal would be more than enough for him. 'What do you usually do on a Sunday afternoon?'

He shrugged. 'Work. Being wealthy isn't all parties and holidays on private yachts, Miranda,' he added as her eyes widened in surprise. 'Of course it has its benefits, but Midas Enterprises owns and runs multinational companies all over the world, and we employ thousands of people. With all of that comes responsibility, to both those companies and their employees.'

'Poor little rich boy?'

He grimaced at her derision. 'Hard as it might be to believe…sometimes, yes.'

Actually, it wasn't all that hard for Andy to believe at all; she had already realised that with great privilege came even greater responsibility. That no matter how nice it must be to be as rich as Darius and Xander Sterne so obviously were, to be able to buy what they wanted, and do whatever they wanted, that they couldn't necessarily do it *when* they wanted. That they might be seen to play hard, but they also had to work hard, in order to run those companies they owned all over the world, and in turn continue to provide thousands of other people with their own livelihoods.

She stood up. 'Then I suggest we leave clearing away the rest of this for now, and instead go to the park over the road and walk off lunch. We can choose a film to watch together when we get back. Does that sound a good plan to you?'

'A walk in the park?'

Andy grinned as she heard the doubt in his voice. 'I'm sure you've heard of it, Darius. You place one foot in front of the other and—'

'I know what walking is, Miranda. I can just think of a more enjoyable form of exercise!' He eyed her expectantly.

'And breathe in the fresh air,' Andy continued with determination even as her cheeks warmed as the gleam in his eyes told her exactly what form of exercise Darius would prefer! 'Admire the flowers, watch the ducks in the pond, the people walking their dogs, and the kids playing on the swings and slides. It's what us less privileged people do for fun after lunch on a warm and sunny Sunday afternoon.'

'Very funny.'

She chuckled as she reached up a hand and pulled the confining band from her hair, allowing its silky straightness to fall about her shoulders. 'Stop grumbling and let's go!' She slipped her bare feet into a pair of ballet pumps near the door.

'You're awfully bossy today.'

She quirked a blonde brow. 'You really shouldn't complain when I've just cooked you lunch.'

'I'm not complaining. Surprisingly, I think I like it.' Darius stepped close enough for Andy to be able to feel the heat of his body. 'Are you this forceful in bed too?'

Andy felt a quiver of awareness run the length of her spine as the huskiness of his voice caressed all the way to her core. Her breasts tingled with sensitivity, the nipples hardening and pressing against the soft material of her bra, and an aching warmth spread between her thighs. 'I...' She cleared her throat as her voice came out as a croak. 'Could we just go for that walk now?' she snapped impatiently.

Darius was still chuckling about her reaction as they left the apartment before crossing over the road to enter the park.

Andy's complete awareness of Darius wasn't helped by the fact that he insisted on holding her hand, his fingers laced intimately with hers, as they strolled through the park together.

'*Now* do we get to enjoy my form of exercise?' Darius murmured an hour or so later, as he turned to take Miranda in his arms the moment the two of them had re-entered her apartment.

'Darius...'

'I've been suffering the torments of hell for hours as I watched the way your jeans hug the tautness of your bottom and imagined your breasts beneath that over-large T-shirt,' he groaned.

'I don't think that's appropriate, Darius.'

'Has anyone ever told you that you think far too much?' He raised his hand to cup one side of her now heated face, the soft pad of his thumb moving lightly across the fullness of her bottom lip.

'Has anyone told you that *you* don't think enough?' she countered. 'Today, our lunch, the walk in the park, was as far as this goes for us, Darius, so let's not do anything that might complicate things, hmm?' she continued with determination. 'We both know there's absolutely no reason we need ever meet each other again after today.'

His eyes narrowed, his jaw tensed. 'I don't like that idea.'

'Tough.' She grimaced.

Darius looked down at her searchingly. Her windswept hair framed the delicate beauty of her face: those sparkling and long-lashed green eyes, the flush to her cheeks, those oh-so-kissable lips so soft beneath his caressing thumb. Her neck was gracefully slender, deep hollows visible at the base of her throat. Her nipples were erect and visibly aroused as they pressed against her T-shirt.

The warmth of his gaze returned to her flushed face. 'I'm going to kiss you now, Miranda. And you're going to let me,' he added firmly as she seemed about to protest.

Letting Darius kiss her wasn't what worried Andy—well, it worried her, but only because she had no idea where it would end. Or if it would end at all…

He continued to hold her gaze, his eyes seductively slumberous and warm and holding Andy captive as his head lowered towards hers.

Her lips parted, her breath leaving her in the softness of a sigh at the first touch of Darius's mouth against hers; her body melted instinctively into his even as her arms moved about his muscled waist to feel the flexing of the muscles in his back as her hands moved beneath his T-shirt, and she touched the warmth of the bare flesh beneath.

'Oh, yes, Miranda, I want your hands on me,' he encouraged gruffly, his breath warm as his lips now travelled across the smoothness of Andy's cheek and down the arched column of her throat, sipping, tasting, gently biting, followed by the moist rasp of his tongue against that sensitised flesh. 'I've longed to do this since the moment I first met you.' His mouth captured hers once again, more fiercely this time. 'And I've *ached* to finish what we started last night.'

Andy's half-hearted protest died in her throat as Darius's hands cupped the cheeks of her bottom and he lifted her up so that her feet no longer touched the ground. She knew that everything that had gone before had all been leading up to this. To this moment.

Andy entwined her legs about his waist and the thickness of his arousal now pressed long and hot against her heated core, before his hips moved in slow and sensual arousal against her as he carried her over to the sofa before sitting down.

Her legs were draped either side of him as the kiss deepened, grew hungrier still as they took from each other, her knees resting on the sofa cushions as she straddled his thighs, pressing that lengthy hardness deeper against and into her, as her arms moved up over his shoulders and her fingers became entangled in the heavy thickness of the dark hair at his nape.

She groaned as Darius's tongue licked

across her parted lips, tasting, sensitising, before invading the heat beneath in a claiming sweep, his tongue a sensual caress as it stroked against hers, slowly at first, and then more demandingly as his hands moved beneath her T-shirt to unfasten her bra and cup her bared breasts.

Her back arched instinctively at the feel of Darius's hands on her sensitive skin; she broke the kiss to give a pleasurable gasp as he captured her nipples between fingers and thumbs, her arousal increasing as he rolled and then lightly pinched those engorged tips.

'This has to come off!' Darius pulled her T-shirt up and then tugged it over Miranda's head to remove it completely before throwing it and her unfastened bra aside, his eyes feeling hot and heavy as he gazed down at her bared breasts.

A lifetime of exercise meant her breasts were small, but perfectly formed, and he cupped a hand beneath each perfect up-tilting mound, enjoying the touch of her silky soft skin as he caressed and squeezed her before slowly lowering his head to capture a nipple into the heat of his mouth.

It took every effort of will on his part not to suckle greedily. He wanted to take this slowly, to savour and enjoy every single moment of making love with Miranda.

To show her that there was *every* reason why the two of them should—and would—meet again.

He sucked gently on her nipple, taking the time to taste her thoroughly, even as his tongue lathed and rasped across it. He was instantly rewarded by Miranda's soft mewls of pleasure as her fingers clung to his shoulders and she arched into him, wanting more, *demanding* more.

Darius gave it to her as he captured her swollen breast in his hand before turning the attention of his tongue and teeth to its twin. He suckled hard as he drew as much of that breast into the heat of his mouth as he could, even as he rolled the length of his arousal up and into the heat between her thighs.

He groaned low in his throat, suckling deeper, harder, as he felt his own pleasure intensify, knowing he too wanted more, that he needed more.

Andy was completely lost to the pleasure of Darius's hands and mouth on her breasts, and the hardness of his arousal pressing remorselessly against her. The pleasure built higher and higher as Darius continued to suckle and caress her, her body aching to be fulfilled.

'Darius, I need—more.' She moved restlessly against him, desperately seeking, needing him to press harder against that aching throb between her thighs. 'Darius, please, I *need*…!'

His lips and tongue eased the pressure on her breast as he raised his head to look at her. 'Tell me,' he encouraged raggedly as his tongue now gently laved her swollen and rosy nipples. 'Tell me what you need, Miranda!' he encouraged fiercely as she made no reply.

Andy breathed shallowly as she undulated her hips against the hardness of his arousal, needing that contact, craving it as she was once again held captive by eyes that were now a deep, dark amber.

'Words, Miranda,' he encouraged throatily, the visible flush against the harshness of his cheekbones telling of his own desire. 'I need to hear the words.'

She moistened the dryness of her lips. 'I don't—'

'Tell me!' His arms tightened about her.

She closed her eyes briefly before opening them again. 'I need you to touch me,' she groaned pleadingly. 'I ache, Darius.'

'Where?'

'Everywhere,' she breathed agitatedly. 'My breasts. Between my legs. Everywhere—' She broke off as Darius's hands once again cupped and lifted beneath her bottom, turning her so that she now lay full length on the sofa as he unfastened the button and zip on her jeans.

Which was when Andy *remembered* and began to panic, her hands moving to cover his in order to stop him from going any further.

'I already know about the scars, Miranda,' he spoke softly.

Andy stilled, hardly daring to breathe, sure her heart had ceased to beat too as she gazed up at him with wide and stricken eyes. 'How could you possibly know?'

'Logic.' Darius gently removed her now un-resisting hands before he continued to fully unzip, and then peel her jeans down to her thighs and further down her legs. 'Your injuries in the accident were extensive.'

'It wasn't…' Andy stopped her protest as she realised she had once again been about to claim that her fall four years ago hadn't been an accident at all; no one had believed her then, and the last thing she needed right now was for Darius to think she was a bitter and twisted hysteric.

'They would also have required several operations, painful ones,' Darius guessed grimly. 'Coupled with Tia Bellamy's comments last night, about the ankle length of your gown, it isn't difficult to guess that you have scars.'

He had managed to pull her jeans down the rest of the way as they talked, and he now discarded them completely, his breath catching in his throat as he turned back and saw that Miranda wore only cream silk and lace bikini briefs beneath. Her golden curls were visible against the dampened silk.

And the scars were visible high up on her right thigh—a delicate tracery of surgical incisions that had faded to silver during the past four years, but were still visible nonetheless.

They were scars Miranda now attempted to hide with her hand. 'They're hideous.'

'They're a part of who you are,' Darius corrected gruffly. 'Like war wounds,' he added softly as he lowered his head and placed his lips gently on each and every one of those scars.

Andy made a choking noise in her throat. 'Darius!'

He continued to kiss her scarred thigh as he murmured, 'We all carry scars, Miranda. Some are visible, others not, but never doubt that we all bear scars from our past.'

Andy heard the bleakness underlying Darius's tone, and wondered what scars he carried around inside him. Recalling the conversation between the two brothers the evening before, it wasn't difficult to realise that it probably somehow involved the father Xander had described as a bastard. It was—

She gave a gasp, all other thoughts leaving her head, as Darius now hooked his thumbs into her lacy briefs and slowly, purposefully, slid them downwards, until he had her completely naked. Her breath caught and held, the heated warmth colouring her cheeks, as he nudged her legs apart before moving to kneel between her thighs, spreading her legs even further apart as he gazed his fill.

'Beautiful,' Darius finally breathed huskily before looking up at her. 'You're beautiful, Miranda. All of you.'

Miranda squirmed uncomfortably. 'I'm feeling a little underdressed.'

Darius clearly heard the embarrassment beneath Miranda's husky tone. 'I believe I'm the one who's a lot overdressed,' he corrected as he reached for the bottom of his T-shirt and drew it up and over his head before throwing it onto the pile of her clothes already gathered on the floor. 'Better?'

Andy totally forgot her embarrassment as she looked at Darius's bared and lightly tanned torso. She drank in his wide and muscled shoulders and chest, defined abs, with not an ounce of superfluous flesh anywhere, testament to the fact that he didn't spend all of his time behind a desk. There was a dusting of dark hair covering the middle of his chest and tapering down beneath the waistband of his jeans. *He* was the one who was beautiful, mouth-wateringly so.

'I'm going to taste you now, Miranda,' he growled hungrily in warning even as he slid down the couch until he was settled between her thighs, the width of his shoulders forcing her legs even further apart.

'I— Oh, dear Lord...!' Andy groaned as she felt Darius's tongue sweep slowly over her, gasping as he hummed his pleasure.

She couldn't resist looking down at him, so dark and primal against her fairness, his lids closed, dark lashes fanning the sharp planes of his cheeks.

Andy's fingers curled into the darkness of his hair as she thought she might die from the pleasure of his lips and tongue.

'I need you to touch me too, Miranda,' he encouraged as he moved up onto his knees, unfastening the button and zip of his jeans and pulling them down.

Andy was thrilled to see his excitement and to know that she was the cause of his arousal. She hesitated only briefly before her fingers closed about his length, amazed at how soft the skin was that encased the steel hardness beneath. Instinctively she moved her hand up and over, mimicking the rhythm he had resumed as he continued to caress her with his tongue.

'Harder, Miranda,' he paused to groan achingly. 'Faster.'

She drew her breath in sharply, her fingers tightening about him, squeezing harder, as Darius's mouth closed completely about her and he suckled deeply, at the same time as he slid first one and then a second finger deep inside her.

Her pleasure rose higher still, threatening to consume her as it rose to a crescendo. Higher, and then higher still, until Andy felt that wave hold, crest, before exploding in a kaleidoscope of sensations, emotions and colours that left her gasping.

Beneath her hand she felt Darius harden before he joined her in his own shuddering climax.

Darius was breathing heavily as he lay against Miranda's thighs, too physically satiated to want to move. Instead he simply enjoyed the pleasure of having her fingers moving caressingly through his hair as she lay just as relaxed beneath him.

It had never been like this for him before.

So intense. So immediate. To the degree that Darius hadn't been able to control or stem his own pleasure, and he'd experienced the deepest and most intense climax of his life.

Damn it, the two of them had made out on Miranda's sofa like a couple of teenagers!

Darius might have laughed at himself for that adolescent eagerness if he weren't so bemused by it.

Not just bemused, utterly confused.

He'd been sexually active since he was in his teens and had always enjoyed sex as a recreation, a release of tension, but this—this time with Miranda had been unlike anything he had ever known before.

He'd felt a connection, the emotions so intense, he had been unable to stop himself from climaxing in her hand like that overeager teenager. And he hadn't even been inside her yet!

A fact his body was only too well aware of, if the stirring of renewed arousal was any indication.

What did it mean?

What did he *want* it to mean?

He liked Miranda. Admired her even. But was it more than that? Could it *be* more than that?

How was he supposed to *think*, about anything, when Miranda still lay naked beneath him, and with the smell of her feminine musk invading, capturing, all of his senses?

Distance.

He needed distance.

Between himself and Miranda.

Except he couldn't think of any way, any graceful way that was, to extricate himself from between her naked thighs, let alone from her apartment!

For goodness' sake, he was Darius Sterne, billionaire businessman, well known for keeping his emotional distance from all but his twin Xander—to the point that several of the women he had been physically involved with in the past had accused him of being cold and ruthless.

But he freely admitted that he had no idea right now how to escape this situation without hurting Miranda. And he didn't want to hurt her; he just needed to get away from her for long enough to be able to think straight. To be able to bring some perspective to the situation. To see if there was any perspective to be found!

The question was how?

This was also something which had certainly never bothered him in the past.

He didn't believe himself to be a deliberately cruel man when it came to the women he had been involved with, he had just never been interested in them outside the bedroom.

He already knew that Miranda wasn't anything like the women he usually slept with. She was nothing like the models and actresses he usually took to bed. They were women who were only too willing to sleep with him, even if for nothing more than the boost the publicity of just being seen out with one of the Sterne brothers could and would give to her career.

Had he always chosen women who were deliberately no threat to his closed-off heart?

Maybe.

But Miranda was different.

He'd had to blackmail Miranda into going out with him at all!

He sensed that she was extremely vulnerable, emotionally as well as physically, and his own emotional scars from the past, and the estrangement between his mother and himself, made him the very last man she should ever become involved with.

Which was why Darius needed to leave.

Now!

He pulled away from her, deliberately not looking at her nakedness as he rose to his feet, knowing that if he did his resolve would weaken, and he would simply end up making love with her again.

'Bathroom?' he prompted gruffly as he re-fastened his jeans before pulling his T-shirt back on.

Darius's thought were an enigma to Andy, but the fact that he couldn't even look at her as he dressed didn't bode well for what he might have been planning in his head for these past few moments.

Which was fine, because Andy couldn't look at him either, now that the euphoria and pleasure had faded and the stark reality of the fact that she had just made love with Darius on her own sofa became all too embarrassingly apparent.

She had never had a man caress her so intimately before. It made her blush just to think of what she and Darius had just enjoyed together!

At the same time as she couldn't forget the ecstasy he'd brought her. It was a pleasure such as Andy had never dreamed possible, let alone ever imagined sharing with Darius Sterne.

He might be physically and emotionally distant now, but he hadn't been at all the cold lover she had feared he would be. No, he had been so considerate of her, so caring of her physical shyness. He had even kissed the scars she had hidden away these past four years!

Which, Andy admitted, had been her complete undoing.

How could she have resisted a man who saw those scars as battle wounds rather than the unsightly imperfection Andy had always considered them to be?

She couldn't. She hadn't wanted to.

And Darius had made her first physical encounter so beautiful.

Enough so that she could feel herself falling in love with him?

Whatever her own feelings on the matter, Darius's distant behaviour told her that the closeness was over.

'Up the stairs and on the right,' she answered him huskily, frowning as Darius turned abruptly on his heel and strode off in the direction of the bathroom without so much as glancing back.

It gave Andy time to quickly gather up her scattered clothes, so that she could dress before Darius came back. Except, she realised as soon as she sat up, that there was no way she could put her clothes back on when her thighs and abdomen still bore the evidence of Darius's climax.

How embarrassing was that!

Maybe if she made a quick run for the kitchen, grabbed a towel, and—

Before she could so much as move Darius had come back out of the bathroom and run lightly down the half a dozen steps onto the main floor space. He was carrying one of her fluffy gold bath towels in his hand, his eyes unreadable as he strode purposefully towards her.

Suddenly acutely aware of her nakedness she instinctively crossed one knee over the other before she leant forward with her elbow on her knee, effectively shielding at least part of her nakedness from him.

'Here.'

The expression in his eyes was hidden behind hooded lids as he handed her the towel before turning away again, shoulders hunched as he thrust his hands into the pockets of jeans. With his back to her he gave Andy the privacy she needed to use the towel before pulling her clothes back on.

'Do we need to talk about this?'

The fact that he needed to ask, and the *way* in which he asked, told Andy that what Darius was actually saying was that *he* didn't want to talk about it.

That he regretted what had happened.

Andy wasn't sure how she felt about what

their lovemaking had revealed to her. But no doubt she would have days and weeks in which to agonise over her feelings.

When she would never hear from Darius again.

Which, Andy realised, saddened her more than she liked to admit.

She had tried from the first to resist her attraction to Darius, knew from their first meeting, when she had been so instantly aware of him that it was a foolish attraction at best, and a dangerous one at worst. An attraction she had guessed would only bring her heartache.

She now knew for certain that it would.

Because her reaction to Darius today, and their lovemaking just now, told her that she had allowed her heart to become involved. She had no idea if that tumult of emotions was actually love, but she definitely had strong feelings for Darius, much stronger feelings than she had ever felt for any other man. Strong enough that she had allowed him to see her scars. That she had then given herself to him willingly.

She hadn't really needed to read all that stuff online about Darius, regarding the history of his brief physical relationships with beautiful models and actresses, to know that he wasn't the type of man who did emotional relationships.

Any more than Andy was a woman who did purely physical ones.

Although Darius certainly couldn't be blamed for thinking that she was, after the way she had behaved with him just now.

The best that she could hope for now was to try to salvage at least some of her pride.

She stood up. 'So...' She frowned at the sound of a mobile phone ringing. It wasn't hers.

Darius muttered under his breath as he drew his mobile from the back pocket of his jeans, a frown between his eyes as he checked the number on the screen. 'I'm sorry but I have to take this.'

Andy nodded abruptly as she turned away to finish tidying up the kitchen, leaving Darius the privacy to take his call. Or at least it started out that way.

'What the—? When?' he demanded of the caller harshly. 'I'll be there as soon as I can. Tell Xander... Never mind, I'll tell him myself when I get there.' He ended the call abruptly. 'I have to leave immediately, Miranda.' He sounded distracted.

Andy had already guessed that much from Darius's half of the conversation. 'Is everything okay? Well, obviously it isn't.' She grimaced. 'What's happened to Xander?' She watched Darius closely, easily noting the pallor of his cheeks, and the shadows in his eyes.

He frowned grimly. 'He was involved in a car accident during the early hours of this morning, but the hospital had no idea who to contact until he regained consciousness a short time ago and could tell them my mobile number.'

Andy took a step towards him, only to come to an abrupt halt as she recognised that at some time over the past thirty seconds he had placed an invisible wall about himself, and one which she couldn't penetrate. 'Is he going to be okay?'

'Let's hope so.' Darius intended to find out the details of Xander's injuries for himself later; for the moment it was enough to take in that his twin was injured and in the hospital. 'I really do have to go to him, Miranda.'

'Well, of course you do,' she accepted briskly.

Earlier Darius had wanted—needed—to put some distance between them, if only so that he could clear his head enough to try and work out what the hell had happened here today. But he certainly hadn't wanted to leave under these circumstances.

The sooner Darius could get to the hospital, and see his twin for himself, the better he would like it.

'Would you like me to drive you to the hospital?'

Darius looked up sharply. 'Sorry?'

'I asked if you would like me to drive you to the hospital,' Andy repeated softly.

'Why?' He looked totally bewildered by the offer.

'It's what friends do for each other, Darius.'

'Is it?'

'Yes. Besides—' she avoided meeting his piercing gaze '—you're obviously upset, and probably shouldn't be driving at the moment.'

He continued to frown as he gave a slow shake of his head. 'I'm going to need my car later...'

'Then I'll drive you there in your car and get a taxi back. Look, I'm not asking any longer, Darius, I'm *telling you* I'm driving you to the hospital,' she added briskly. An uncertain Darius was definitely out of character. 'What happens after that will be completely up to you.'

Although she already had a feeling that she wouldn't be seeing Darius again after today.

CHAPTER EIGHT

DARIUS KNEW HE'D had every reason to feel concerned about his twin as he looked down at Xander lying asleep in the hospital bed. His brother's face was deathly pale apart from a colourful bruise on his brow from where his head had struck the windscreen. The doctor had taken Darius aside in the corridor and informed him that they were currently monitoring Xander for concussion, that his ribs were badly bruised, and his left leg had been badly broken, and required surgery.

Xander's lashes flickered several times before his lids were slowly raised and he looked up at Darius with dark and pain-filled eyes.

'What the hell did you think you were doing?' Darius's voice sounded harsh in the otherwise silence of the room, his hands clenched at his sides. 'I realise you've been acting more recklessly than usual this past few months but not to the point of nearly killing yourself.'

'Darius,' Andy remonstrated gently, knowing it was worry for his twin that motivated his anger, and that he would probably regret this outburst later if it wasn't stopped now.

Darius had been tensely silent on the drive over to the hospital, offering no objection when Andy got out of the car with the intention of accompanying him inside. Not, she had realised, because he had actually wanted her with him, but because he was so distracted and worried about his brother that he had simply forgotten she was there.

Her heart melted now as she saw the desolation in Darius's expression as he looked down at her blankly.

'I'm not suicidal, Darius,' Xander spoke huskily, as if it hurt to do so. Which it probably did, when his ribs were badly bruised. 'I just… I went on to the club late last night and something happened, Darius.' Xander's voice cracked, dark eyes glistening with emotion. 'Something so—I lost control, Darius!' He gave a pained groan. 'I lost control, and I never wanted to be like *him*!'

'Him?' Darius repeated cautiously.

'Our father!' Xander snapped angrily. 'I don't want—I never want to be him.'

'You aren't in the least like him,' Darius cut in harshly. 'And you never could be.'

'But—'

'You are nothing like him, Xander,' Darius insisted firmly. 'If you lost control then you had a damned good reason for doing so, I'm sure,' he added grimly.

Xander gave a shake of his head. 'There's no excuse for the way I behaved.'

'There is!' Darius's hands were once again clenched at his sides. 'There must be,' he insisted firmly.

Xander's expression softened. 'I want to believe that, but…'

'But nothing,' his twin dismissed bleakly. 'Xander, we both suffered at his hands, you physically, and me— Do you have any idea of the guilt I've carried around all these years?'

Xander visibly swallowed. 'Guilt?'

'Yes, damn it, because I was the one he didn't hit!' Darius moved restlessly away from the bed, his face as pale as his twin's. 'So many times I tried to draw his attention away from you, but it never worked.' He drew in a ragged breath. 'And all these years I've wondered if I could have done something differently. If I had maybe just…'

'It wasn't your fault, Darius,' Xander reassured him gruffly.

'It always felt as if it was!' He breathed

heavily. 'That last time he hit you—I just wanted it to stop, Xander. For *him* to stop!'

'I know, Darius.' His twin spoke softly. 'Mother and I have always known, but been too afraid to ask, to confirm, our suspicions. I've dealt with it by ignoring it, and Mother has dealt with it by a "don't ask, don't tell" policy that has resulted in the two of you barely speaking to each other unless it's absolutely necessary.'

'Dealt with what?' Darius looked baffled.

Andy had been feeling decidedly uncomfortable these past few minutes, knowing she was intruding on a very private conversation between the two brothers, and that she was learning much more about the Sterne twins than Darius would thank her for when he was feeling less emotional. 'I think I should go now and leave the two of you to talk,' she put in softly.

The brothers both turned to look at her blankly, confirming they had both forgotten she was there.

'When, or if, you have the time, could I ask that you call me to let me know how Xander is?' she now asked Darius gently before turning to smile at Xander. 'And you just concentrate on getting better, hmm?' she encouraged huskily. 'Your brother loves you very much.'

Xander's smile was bleak. 'I know.'

'I'll walk you out, Miranda,' Darius stated evenly.

'There's no need, really.'

'There's every need,' he insisted firmly. 'I'll be back in a few minutes,' he assured Xander before following Andy from the room. 'I'm sorry you had to hear any of that,' he said gruffly once they were outside in the hospital corridor.

Andy wasn't. The conversation between the two brothers had been very revealing. And it confirmed, she believed, that the way Darius distanced himself from others, and his difficult relationship with his mother, all stemmed from a childhood spent with what now sounded like an abusive father, and a mother who preferred not to talk about it after the death of her husband.

She placed her hand on Darius's arm. 'You and Xander need to talk.'

'It seems that we do.' He nodded grimly. 'I— Thank you for driving me here today, Miranda. I appreciate it more than I can tell you. I'll talk to you again when I've sorted this mess out.'

'Don't worry about me, Darius,' Andy hastened to reassure him, not wanting him to feel as if he had to contact her, be with her, again.

'Just concentrate on sorting out your relationship with Xander and your mother.'

He grimaced. 'It sounds pretty messed up, hmm?'

'It sounds…complicated. But if anyone can resolve it, you can,' she added reassuringly.

'I admire your confidence in my abilities—' he smiled bleakly '—but it sounds as if I should have done that years ago.'

Andy squeezed his arm. 'Then you'll do it now.'

Darius looked down at her. 'You really believe that, don't you?'

She smiled. 'You're Darius Sterne. Of course I believe it.'

He took both of her hands in his much larger ones. 'And you're Miranda Jacobs. And you should dance again.'

'What?' Andy gave him a frowning glance.

'You should dance at my mother's gala, Miranda,' he told her gruffly.

She swallowed. 'I don't think…' She gave a slightly dazed shake of her head. 'I'll think about it.'

'Good.' He gave her hands a squeeze before releasing them and stepping back. 'I'll call you later,' he promised.

* * *

'Mother, I wanted to talk to you about—Miranda?'

Andy had given a start at the unexpected sound of Darius's voice, her hands starting to shake and causing the fine china teacup to rattle in its saucer, as she turned to look at him across Catherine Latimer's elegantly decorated blue and cream drawing room.

It had been five days since Sunday night when Darius had called her and reassured her that the doctors had said that Xander would eventually make a full recovery.

Since then there had been only silence between them.

And it wasn't too difficult to guess why.

Andy had known at the time that Darius wouldn't thank her for overhearing that conversation between himself and Xander.

Although she doubted that was the only reason for Darius's silence.

The two of them had made love last Sunday, and the fact that Darius hadn't contacted her since seemed to indicate he now regretted it. As Andy had suspected he might. He might have desired her, wanted to make love to her, but she really wasn't his type.

Looking at Darius now, dressed in one of

those exquisite business suits he habitually wore, made it hard for Andy to believe he was the same man who had made love to her the previous weekend.

Difficult, but not impossible, as the heated awareness now suffusing Andy's body testified!

Caught up now, as she was, in the direct glow of his eyes, Andy couldn't have answered his question at that moment if her life had depended upon it.

Darius strolled further into the drawing room, his narrowed gaze fixed firmly on her. 'Miranda?' he repeated huskily.

Andy carefully placed her teacup down on the coffee table before standing up, her legs trembling as she did so. Seeing Darius again so unexpectedly had thrown her completely.

She was relieved she had at least worn a formal pale green blouse, tucked into tailored black trousers, for this arranged meeting today with Catherine Latimer. Her hair was also newly washed and styled, so she could at least meet Darius on an equal footing in regard to her appearance.

She turned to smile reassuringly at the older woman. 'I think we've said all we need to say for today, Catherine, so I'll leave you alone to talk with your son now.'

Pleasure shone in the older woman's eyes. 'I can't tell you how pleased I am that you've changed your mind.'

Darius might now regret their intimacies of the previous weekend, but that didn't mean that Andy hadn't listened to him at the hospital when he had suggested she should dance at the gala his mother was organising. Especially when he had been so confident that she could.

Determined not to dwell on thoughts of Darius, of what he meant to her, Andy had instead agonised about whether or not she could dance again in public. Was she was emotionally strong enough to do so, as well as physically?

Darius's confidence in her had been the deciding factor in all that agonising. He believed in her. Believed she could do it.

Her visit to Catherine Latimer today, to accept her invitation to dance at the gala, was the result of all that agonising.

Although she didn't think now was the time for her to talk about that decision with Darius.

Andy glanced across at the glowering Darius. 'I really do have to go now. No, please don't bother to call the butler,' she added hastily as Catherine would have summoned the middle-aged retainer who had shown her into the drawing room earlier. 'It's a nice day, so

I didn't bring a coat, and I can find my own way out.'

Darius was still so stunned at finding Miranda here that he was only half listening to the conversation between his mother and his—wait, what exactly was Miranda to him? His *lover?* Because there was no doubt in his mind, despite the fact that he deliberately hadn't seen or spoken to her since last Sunday, that that was exactly what she was.

And she had been positively the last person he had been expecting to see when he'd called to see his mother this morning!

So much so that he couldn't even think of the words to now stop Miranda from leaving as she moved quietly past him before exiting the drawing room and stepping out into the hallway.

Andy gratefully breathed the fresh spring air into her lungs once she stood on the top step outside the house, leaning back gratefully on the front door of the Latimers' London home, her knees feeling suddenly weak.

Despite her hopes that Darius and his mother had healed the long-held rift between them, Darius had still been the last person Andy had expected to see today.

It was a shock that had so obviously been

mutual. Darius had looked as stunned to see her as she was to—

Andy almost fell backwards into the house as the front door was wrenched open behind her, and she fought to retain her balance even as she turned to face Darius.

She instantly raised her chin defensively. 'I know how strange this must look to you, but I assure you my visit to your mother this morning has absolutely nothing to do with you.'

Darius smiled as a five-day-long heaviness seemed to lift from his chest. 'I never for a moment assumed that it did.'

'No?' There was still that challenging spark in her eyes.

Darius tilted his head. 'Are you angry with me?'

Andy opened her mouth, and then closed it again, as she realised she *was* angry. And hurt.

This man had made love to her last Sunday, and apart from a brief—very brief—telephone call late on Sunday evening Andy hadn't heard another word from him since. About anything.

The newspapers had been full of the story of Xander Sterne's car accident this past week, describing his injuries as extensive. Obviously the press were prone to exaggeration, but when Andy had enquired after Xander this morning Catherine Latimer had assured her that Xander would only be in the private clinic for a few more days.

But Andy knew it wasn't Darius's silence regarding his brother that hurt her.

She had *known* after their lovemaking on Sunday that she would never mean anything more to Darius than those brief moments of pleasure. And his silence these past five days had only confirmed that. It hurt so much.

Oh, she hadn't fooled herself for a minute into believing that their lovemaking meant any more to him than had the legion of other women he had taken to bed over the past fifteen years. But she hadn't realised just how much it would hurt not to receive so much as even a courtesy phone call from him this past week. His complete silence had just been insulting.

She drew in a deep breath. 'I have to go. I have a class in a little under an hour.'

Darius frowned. Okay, so his emotions had been so—so confused these past five days that he had made a conscious decision not to call Miranda again until he knew what was going on in his head, but that didn't mean he hadn't thought about her constantly since Sunday. That he hadn't relived and enjoyed, over and over again, the memories of the two of them making love together. Or that he hadn't puzzled over exactly why that was. And what it meant…

Because he had done all of those things.

And he had also known when he'd got out of bed this morning, after another restless night's sleep thinking about her, that this couldn't go on any longer, that he needed to see her again, to kiss her, to make love to her. He had fully intended to see Miranda later today.

Walking into his mother's home and finding Miranda calmly drinking tea from one of his mother's twee china cups had been the last thing he had expected!

He gazed down at her hungrily now through narrowed lids and he knew exactly why he had so badly needed to see and be with her again.

'I would love to stand here and talk to you all morning,' she now told Darius with ill-concealed insincerity as she gave an impatient glance down at her wristwatch, 'but I really do have a class in just under an hour. And you're obviously here to visit your mother,' she reminded him.

'You and I need to talk.'

'Some other time,' she dismissed distractedly, her smile bright and meaningless as she turned to go down the rest of the steps and along the path towards the metal gate leading out onto the street.

Darius watched in frustration the gentle sway of Miranda's hips as she let herself out of the gate before turning and walking the short distance to where her car was parked further down the street. She unlocked the door and got in behind the wheel before turning on the engine and driving away.

All without so much as giving him even the briefest backward glance, and the contained expression on Miranda's face as she drove away told him that she had already dismissed him.

His first instinct was to follow her right now, and demand that she finish their conversation. He also intuited that Miranda didn't want to talk to him.

Well, to hell with that!

The two of them needed to talk. Not least about the conversation she had overheard at the hospital a week ago between himself and Xander.

'So this is your little dance studio…'

Andy had been in the middle of her limbering down routine, following her late morning class, but she turned sharply now to look across the studio to where Tia Bellamy posed elegantly in the doorway.

Tia looked as beautiful as ever, in a fitted black dress, and four-inch-heeled strappy sandals—instantly making Andy aware of how dishevelled and sweaty she was in her leotard, the dampness of her hair confined in a topknot, the flatness of her ballet shoes also making her several inches shorter than Tia.

Deliberately so?

Probably, Andy conceded heavily as she picked up a towel and draped it about the dampness of her neck and shoulders, before answering the other woman. 'Yes, this is my dance studio.'

Blue eyes swept over the mirrored room contemptuously, that gaze no less condescending as it returned to Andy. 'I suppose it's one way to make a living.'

'I suppose it is,' Andy echoed wryly; the gloves definitely appeared to be off today. Not such a surprise, when there was no male audience for Tia to play to! 'What can I do for you, Tia?' she enquired briskly as she tidied the benches along one wall, picking up a stray towel here and there ready for the laundry. 'I take it this isn't a social call?'

'Hardly, when you and I were never friends

to begin with.' Tia made no attempt to hide her disdain.

Andy gave her a considering look. 'Why *was* that? What was it about me that you disliked from the moment we were first introduced?'

'Don't be naive, Andy,' the older woman replied sharply.

'I'm not.' Andy's expression was genuinely perplexed as she gave a shake of her head. 'I truly have no idea what I ever did to you to make you dislike me so much.'

Blue eyes narrowed viciously. 'You *existed*!'

Andy's breath caught at the back of her throat at the sound of the other woman's vitriol. 'I don't understand.'

'Of course you don't.' Tia continued to glare at her. 'You were such a little innocent it never even occurred to you that I was older than you, more senior than you in the ballet company, and that it should have been *me* who was chosen to dance the lead in *Giselle* and *Swan Lake*, rather than being chosen as your understudy.'

'It wasn't—I wasn't responsible for making those choices.' Andy gave a dazed shake of her head.

Tia snorted scornfully. 'Oh, everyone talked for months about how wonderful you were—

the ballet company, other dancers, the public. You were tipped to be the next Fonteyn.' Her top lip curled. 'What a pity you ultimately weren't able to live up to all that potential!'

'That wasn't my fault.'

'Isn't that the age-old cry of every failure that ever lived?' Tia strolled further into the studio, the coldness of her gaze sweeping disparagingly over all that Andy had worked so hard to achieve and build these past years.

Andy remembered what Darius's response had been the night she had called herself a failure. 'I didn't fail, Tia, I just made a career change because of my circumstances.'

Tia gave a smile much like a cat that had lapped up a bowl of cream. 'And what circumstances would those be, Andy?'

Andy let out an impatient sigh. 'Look, Tia, I have absolutely no idea what you're doing here...what possible reason you could have for deliberately seeking me out in this way.' Because, there was no denying it, the other woman *had* come here deliberately. 'But I think it obvious from our brief conversation that we have nothing left to say to each other.'

'You may have nothing to say to me, but I still have plenty of things to say to you,' Tia bit out coldly. 'The main one being that I want you to refuse Catherine Latimer's invitation to dance at the gala next month.'

Andy blinked. 'How could you possibly even know about that?'

'How?' Tia bit out disgustedly. 'Because the stupid woman telephoned me yesterday with the idea, if you agree to perform at all, of asking the two of us to dance together at the finale after dancing individually. *I* am a prima ballerina.' Blue eyes flashed. 'I do not dance with performers who are inferior.'

'It's a charity gala, Tia.'

'That doesn't mean it should be performed by people who are charity cases themselves!'

Andy flinched at the other woman's deliberate cruelty.

Admittedly, she hadn't had a chance to finish her conversation with Catherine Latimer this morning, because of Darius's unexpected arrival, but she had to agree that Catherine's idea, of Tia and Andy dancing on stage together at the end of the gala performance next month, was ludicrous. Even the hours they would necessarily have to spend together rehearsing would be impossible, let alone the two of them actually dancing on stage together in public.

'I'll speak to her.'

'You won't just speak to her—you'll tell her that you aren't going to dance at all.'

'Why would I want to do that?' Andy gave a slow shake of her head. 'I only spoke to Catherine this morning and accepted the invitation,' she explained at Tia's narrow-eyed glare.

Andy had done a lot of soul-searching this past week, in the wake of her lovemaking with Darius, and Xander Sterne's accident.

She could imagine only too well the pain and frustration Xander had gone through this past week. And she knew with certainty that, being Darius's twin, Xander had the will power and determination to recover fully from his injuries.

Just as she had recovered, as much as she was able, from her own injuries four years ago.

Never once in their acquaintance had Darius ever treated her as less because of those injuries that had ended her ballet career. In fact he had done the opposite, and challenged her at every opportunity.

By goading her into dancing with him that first evening. By insisting that she attend the charity dinner with him—her first appearance in public in four years. By kissing each and every one of her scars as they'd made love on Sunday afternoon, telling her he considered them to be the scars from a battle she had fought and won. Which in a way they were. The two of them might not have a future together, but Andy would always be grateful to Darius for his faith in her, for giving her the courage to face her own demons, her fear of failure.

It was Darius's belief in her that had given her the newfound confidence, the courage, to dance in public again. Just a short ten-minute performance—she wasn't capable of anything more—but Andy had determined she *would* do that much.

She was still determined.

Whether Tia liked it or not.

'I suppose I could always arrange for you to have another accident.'

Andy stilled, hardly breathing, the colour having leeched from her cheeks, her eyes wide with shock as she stared across the room at Tia Bellamy.

As Andy digested and analysed what the other woman had just said to her.

'It really *was* you,' she finally managed to say breathily, eyes wide with horror that someone—Tia Bellamy—could actually have done something so horrific to a fellow dancer as push her off the stage.

In contrast, Tia's expression was one of

boredom. 'Of course it was me. As I said, for the second time in a matter of months you were dancing the lead and I was the understudy. A lead that should have been mine—that *became* mine and stayed mine once you were out of the way!' she added triumphantly. 'Now I'm the prima ballerina and you're—well, you're this.' She gave a dismissive sweep of her crimson-tipped fingers at their surroundings.

'But—but—you could have killed me! You did injure me enough that I'll never dance professionally again.' Andy felt physically sick. She might just *be* sick, if she had to be in this woman's company for too much longer. 'I think you had better go,' she advised woodenly.

How could someone *do* that to another person, to another dancer? How could Tia have deliberately pushed Andy off a stage just so that she could take her place? It was evil!

Even the satisfaction of knowing she had been right, after all, four years ago, wasn't enough to quell the sickening churning of Andy's stomach.

'You'll call Catherine Latimer and tell her you've decided not to dance, after all,' Tia instructed.

Would she? Would Andy allow this woman's threats to destroy her life for a second time? Wasn't she more than that? Hadn't Darius's admiration for what she had now made of her life, the desire he had shown for her last weekend, made her more than just her past?

Andy was pretty sure that it had.

'Why would she want to do that?' Darius rasped harshly, drawing Andy's stricken gaze to him as he stood in the open doorway. 'Would someone like to tell me what the hell is going on here?' he added coldly as he stepped into the room, his eyes glittering brightly.

CHAPTER NINE

DARIUS HAD SEEN a car that he knew wasn't Miranda's parked outside the studio, and heard the sound of raised voices as soon as he entered the building. Well…one raised voice—which he now knew to be Tia Bellamy's—followed by Miranda's softer, more measured responses to whatever the other woman was saying to her.

He studied the two women now through narrowed lids, easily taking in the pallor of Miranda's face, her eyes appearing a huge dark green against that paleness, just as Tia Bellamy's face was flushed with anger, her eyes like chips of blue glass as she glared at Miranda.

'Ladies?' he prompted coldly—although he used the term loosely in regard to Tia Bellamy; as far as he could tell there was little that was ladylike about her, no matter how she might try to give the opposite impression.

The ballerina seemed to gather herself together with effort as she shot Miranda one last telling glare before turning to bestow a flirtatious smile on Darius. 'It was nothing important,' she dismissed airily. 'And I have a rehearsal to get to now, so Andy and I will have to finish catching up some other time— What are you doing?' she said sharply, Darius having reached out and grasped the top of her arm to stop her from leaving.

His hold didn't slacken in the slightest. 'Miranda?' he prompted softly.

Andy drew in a deep breath before giving a weary shake of her head. 'Let her go.'

'Are you sure?'

'Very,' she bit out decisively.

Darius's fingers tightened briefly on Tia Bellamy's arm. 'I seriously advise you never to come here and upset Miranda again,' he warned grimly.

Those blue eyes flashed resentfully before Tia reluctantly gave an abrupt nod of her head.

Darius released her, not even sparing her another glance as she left the room. Instead he crossed the room to Miranda's side as the outer door slammed noisily behind Tia Bellamy seconds later. 'Are you okay?' he prompted gently as he placed a hand beneath Miranda's chin and raised her face to his and looked down at her searchingly.

Was she okay?

Tia had just confirmed what Andy had always suspected: that she had deliberately pushed her off the stage four years ago. Which, although a disturbing revelation, had at least reassured Andy that she hadn't imagined it after all.

The other woman had also just issued another veiled warning: to cause Andy further harm if she didn't withdraw from performing at the gala next month.

So was she okay?

Not in the least!

The trembling started in Andy's knees, before travelling through the rest of her body, so that within seconds, it seemed, she was on the brink of collapsing.

'Come and sit down before you fall down.' Darius had placed a firm arm about her waist to hold her against his side as he guided her over to one of the benches against the wall, sitting down and pulling Andy down onto his thighs, resting her head against his shoulder, as his arms came around her protectively.

Which was when Andy's tears began to fall hotly down her cheeks.

Because she now knew for certain that the

shattering of her dream four years ago, of becoming a world-famous ballerina, had been a deliberate and malicious act.

Because of all those years of self-doubt Andy had suffered, when she had sometimes questioned her own sanity, for having even the thought that someone could have deliberately pushed her that night.

To make matters worse, Andy could no longer deny, after seeing Darius again at his mother's house this morning, that she had fallen deeply and irrevocably in love, and with a man she knew had no intentions of ever falling in love with her!

All of which meant that she was now overwhelmed by emotions, made worse by the fact that Darius was the one now holding her so tenderly in his arms.

And it couldn't continue. Even if she liked, loved, the idea of Darius trying to slay dragons for her, she knew she was stronger than that. Much as she might like to lean on him, she was capable of slaying her own dragons.

She drew in a deep, controlling breath and wiped the tears from her cheeks before sitting up, determined not to make any more of a fool of herself than she already had. 'Sorry about that. I think I overreacted slightly,' she attempted to dismiss—and knew she had failed utterly as Darius continued to frown with concern.

'Like to share?' he prompted softly.

Andy chewed briefly on her bottom lip, wondering how much Darius had overheard of her conversation with Tia, and how much more she wanted to reveal to him. Not that Darius would let his questions go unanswered.

'What are you doing here?' she asked instead.

He gave a humourless smile. 'It was always my intention to come and see you this morning.'

She blinked. 'Why?'

'Stop changing the subject, Miranda,' he bit out impatiently. 'I didn't get the impression at the dinner last Saturday evening that you and Tia were exactly friends, so what was she doing here just now? And, more to the point, why did she think she had the right to tell you not to dance at my mother's gala?' He frowned.

Andy avoided meeting his probing gaze. 'It was nothing.'

'It was most definitely something, to have reduced you to tears; you are the least weepy woman I know!'

Andy drew in a shuddering breath; how was she even supposed to think straight when she was sitting on Darius's muscled thighs?

When her senses were all reacting to his warmth and the sensuously earthy smell of his body that was uniquely and arousingly Darius, as well as that insidious lemon and spice aroma of his aftershave?

'Thank you—I think.' She grimaced. 'Look, I've just taken a class, and I'm feeling hot and sticky, so could we go upstairs before we continue with this conversation? That way I can shower and change before making us both some coffee.'

'I would rather we stayed exactly where we are,' Darius rasped.

Andy looked up at him guardedly. 'You would?'

He nodded. 'I have this unrelenting fantasy of making love to you in front of all these mirrors,' he said throatily even as his arms tightened about her.

Andy's eyes widened. 'You do?'

'Oh, yes!' Darius breathed huskily.

Andy wasn't sure she was capable of even standing up after that comment, let alone walking up the stairs to her apartment.

Darius had *fantasised* about making love to her in this room? Since when? An *unrelenting* fantasy? He had only come into the dance studio itself once before today, when he'd invited her to the charity dinner with him, so did that mean he had been fantasising about making love to her in here since then?

The heat in his gaze as he looked down at her seemed to say that he had!

Andy was suddenly aware of how little she was actually wearing, just a white leotard and tights, all of which clung to every curve of her body.

She moistened her lips with the tip of her tongue. 'That sounds…intriguing.'

'It does?'

'Um…yes…' What was the point of her even trying to deny her response to the suggestion, when Darius must be able to feel the sudden warmth between her thighs as she sat on the muscled hardness of his lap. And he couldn't miss that her nipples were aroused and pressed against the thin material of her leotard!

His arms tightened about her as he gave a husky laugh. 'Does that mean you've forgiven me for not contacting you since last Sunday?'

'It means I'm thinking about it,' she came back pertly.

'Dependent on…?'

Andy moved back slightly so that she could look at him, her heart melting at just how devastatingly handsome he looked when he smiled in that relaxed way. 'Dependent upon whether you didn't call me because you didn't want to, or you didn't call me because you wanted to but made yourself not do so.'

The moment of truth, Darius realised, wondering if he was ready for this. Wondering if he would *ever* be ready for this.

He had spent the past twenty years building up the emotional barriers that had protected him from allowing anyone close to him, apart from his twin, as a shield against other people, and the pain of the distance that had so suddenly sprung into existence between himself and his mother.

A distance that, this past week, while still not completely resolved, was no longer that painful mystery to him.

A distance that he had to discuss with Miranda, before he could even begin to answer any other question. Although, after overhearing part of his conversation with Xander at the hospital the previous week, perhaps some of it wouldn't come as such a shock to her?

'Perhaps we should go upstairs to your apartment for coffee, after all.' He now set her lightly on her feet as he stood up, his expression deliberately non-committal as Miranda looked up at him searchingly.

Andy had no idea what to make of Darius's

behaviour: flirtatious one moment, distant and almost businesslike the next.

Disappointed as she was that he obviously no longer intended making love to her right here and right now, she regretted even more that something she had said meant that Darius was no longer relaxed and smiling.

'Fine.' She nodded, leading the way out of the studio, locking the front door to the building before preceding Darius up the stairs to her apartment. Still totally aware of him walking behind her. 'Feel free to put some music on while I take a shower.' She indicated the sound system once they were in her apartment, not meeting his gaze again before turning to go up the short staircase to her bedroom and bathroom.

'Miranda?'

She turned, her expression guarded. 'Yes?'

'I— We...' He gave a shake of his head. 'You're the only woman I've ever known who has been able to render me verbally incompetent!' He ran a frustrated hand through the already tousled darkness of his hair.

Some of Andy's tension left her as she grinned. 'I'll take that as a compliment!'

Darius gave a grimace. 'Oh, it's so much more than that.'

Yes, it was, Andy realised; Darius wasn't

a man who enjoyed admitting to having any sort of weakness, least of all when it came to a woman; no doubt a legacy of his mother's reserve towards him. But *she* had succeeded in rendering him verbally incompetent.

'Make yourself at home while I take a shower,' she invited warmly as she ran lightly up the rest of the stairs to collect some clean clothes before disappearing into the bathroom.

Darius scrolled through her music selection, selecting a random album to play. He removed his jacket and tie and unbuttoned the top button of his shirt before commencing to pace the apartment restlessly.

Half of him wanted to go and join Miranda in the shower—if she would let him—and the more sensible half of him knew they needed to talk about several things before that was even a possibility.

Firstly, he had every intention of discovering the real reason for Tia Bellamy's visit to Miranda. And secondly, he wanted Miranda to know all of the history, not just part of it, of the reason for the estrangement between himself and his mother, and the subsequent effect that history had, and was still having, on Xander.

What happened after that was anyone's guess; Darius knew he was too involved, too *emotionally* involved, to be able to approach the subject of a possible future for himself and Miranda with any of his usual cold logic.

It was—

'How's Xander doing now?'

Darius had been so deep in thought that he hadn't been aware that Miranda had finished in the bathroom and had now rejoined him in the main part of the apartment.

Her hair was no longer confined but soft and silky about her shoulders, her eyes bright and glowing; there was a slight blush of colour in her cheeks, and she was wearing a fitted black T-shirt and jeans.

Darius smiled slightly as he saw that her feet were once again bare. 'You don't do shoes much, do you?'

'Too many years of spending hours in ballet slippers,' she dismissed. 'Shall I make coffee?'

'Not yet.'

'So, how is your brother?' she asked to fill the silence.

'How do you *do* that?' He frowned.

She looked slightly bewildered. 'Do what?'

'Know what I'm thinking about and strike straight to the heart of it?'

'I didn't mean to…' Andy gave Darius a searching glance, noting the shadows in his eyes, the pallor to cheeks so tightly drawn they might have been etched by a sculptor. 'This morning, when I asked your mother about Xander, she didn't seem to think there were going to be any complications with his recovery.'

'From the ribs or broken leg, no.' Darius sighed heavily. 'Unfortunately, as you are already aware, Xander has emotional wounds that may take longer to heal.' He grimaced. 'But we're jumping ahead of ourselves,' he continued briskly. 'I still want to know what that Bellamy woman was doing here, and why she's upset you so much.'

Once again Darius displayed that dogged persistence Andy found so unnerving. A persistence she found she couldn't withstand. 'I don't know if your mother's told you, but I've decided to dance at the gala next month, after all.'

'She did.' His eyes glowed his approval. 'But I thought I would wait for you to tell me before saying anything. I hope this doesn't sound in the least patronising, because it isn't meant to—' he smiled warmly '—but I am so proud of you.'

Andy's breath caught in her throat. 'You are?'

'Oh, yes.' He grinned. 'To the point that I've

already told my mother I'll be joining her and Charles in their box at the theatre that night.'

Her heart skipped a beat at the thought of Darius being part of the audience watching her perform in public for the first time in four years. 'Tia wants me to withdraw from the performance.'

Darius shook his head. 'And what the hell gives her the right to ask you to do anything, let alone something as important as this undoubtedly is?'

'She didn't ask, Darius, she threatened.' Andy lowered her lashes, unable to look up at Darius right now.

Darius became very still as an icy calm settled in his chest. 'Her visit today is only half the story, right?'

Andy drew in a shaky breath as she nodded. 'If you would like to sit down, I'll tell you the rest of it.'

Darius wasn't sure he wanted to sit down—in fact, he knew that he didn't—but Miranda seemed to need him to. And if that was what she needed right now, he wanted to give it to her.

And so he sat and listened, his hands tightening into fists as Miranda told him what had really happened four years ago. How her injury had allowed Tia, as her understudy, to take over the lead in *Swan Lake*. And how Tia had repeated the threat, just now, of further violence if Miranda didn't withdraw from the gala.

Andy couldn't fail to notice the chilling anger in the rigid pallor of Darius's face as she told him Tia had admitted to having deliberately caused her accident four years ago. His eyes took on a cold and dangerously amber glitter as she told him of Tia's renewed threat if she didn't withdraw from the gala.

She took a step back now as Darius surged angrily to his feet the moment she had finished talking. 'I'm not going to withdraw, Darius,' she assured him quickly.

'I wouldn't let you even if you tried,' he bit out harshly, a nerve pulsing in his tightly clenched jaw. 'My God, when I think of how close that woman came to killing you...!' He drew in a shuddering breath as he obviously sought to control the coldness of his temper. 'You have to go to the police with this, Miranda.'

'And tell them what? I have no proof that any of it actually happened, and it will be my word against hers.'

'Don't you see, Miranda? The woman has no conscience, no sense of remorse, no barometer of what's right or wrong.' He stepped forward to grasp both of her hands tightly in his as he looked down at her intently. 'If she was capable of doing this to you to further her own ambitions, then there's no reason to suppose that she hasn't done something similar to others in the past. Or that she won't do so again to others in the future. And possibly next time she won't just ruin someone's career, she might actually succeed in killing them!'

Andy hadn't looked at it in quite that light before. And Darius was right: the Tia who had spoken to her today, threatened her, was totally without conscience, and more than capable of doing whatever it took, whatever was needed, to ensure her own ambitions, whatever they might be.

'We'll do this together,' Darius encouraged huskily. 'And I guarantee that the police will at least listen if I confirm that she threatened you today,' he added grimly. 'Enough to speak with Tia Bellamy, at least.'

'Why would you want to do that for me?'

That moment of truth again, Darius realised.

Except he still hadn't told Miranda about his own past...or explained the continuing repercussions of that past. And he owed it to Miranda to do that, before he dared even think of broaching any sort of future together for the two of them. There was always the possibility she might not want to have anything more to do with him once she knew exactly what a messed-up family he had!

He *would* get to that in a moment; for now he was still so stunned by what Miranda had just told him. 'I still can't believe anyone could deliberately do what Tia Bellamy did to you four years ago.' Reaction was starting to set in now, at the realisation of how close he had come to never meeting Miranda at all. Never knowing her. Never kissing her. Never making love to her. Never falling in love with her...

Because Darius had realised after these few days of forcing himself not to call her, to see her, to be with her, that he did love Miranda. More than anything else. More than his twin. More than any of his family. More than life itself.

His hands clenched at his sides. 'I want to strangle that Bellamy woman with my bare hands for what she did to you!'

'But you won't.' Andy gave a firm shake of her head. 'I've made something else of my life now, Darius. Something I enjoy just as much.' Andy realised even as she said it that it was the truth; she did enjoy teaching ballet—still had the dream of one day discovering her own future Margot Fonteyn or Darcy Bussell. She had a *life*. 'And I've decided that there's absolutely no reason why I can't dance again, just not professionally. But definitely at galas like your mother's—if I'm asked.'

'Oh, don't worry, my mother will ensure that you are,' Darius drawled dryly.

She nodded. 'It's enough.'

'Is it?' Darius looked down at her searchingly, knowing that he wanted more than that, for himself, as well as for Miranda. If she would have him.

It really was time for that moment of truth.

His mouth tightened. 'It's your turn to sit now, and listen to what I need to tell you.'

Andy continued to look at Darius as she made her way slowly over to the sofa and sat down. She could see he was under severe strain, by the dark shadows in his eyes, and the lines grooved beside his eyes and the grimness of his mouth as he restlessly paced the room.

'What is it, Darius?' she finally asked gently when she couldn't stand the suspense any longer. 'Whatever it is, it can't be as bad as the things I've just told you!' she added in an attempt to tease him out of his tension.

'It's worse.' He gave a rueful grimace. 'And it involves the conversation you heard a part of last Sunday at the hospital.'

'Ah.' Andy had wondered if he would ever

talk to her more fully about that. She had wondered this week if he would ever talk to her again!

Darius nodded grimly. 'In particular, my bastard of a father.'

Andy was aware of Xander's distress last Sunday, regarding Lomax Sterne, and she had also realised that Catherine's marriage to the man hadn't exactly been a happy one. She just wasn't sure that Catherine or Xander would thank Darius for discussing that husband, or father, with someone outside their family.

At the same time as she knew that if Darius wanted to talk to her about his father then she would gladly listen.

How could she not?

Darius was a very private man, to the point of obsession. Not cold, as Andy had originally thought him to be—she would never think of him as being cold again, after the way the two of them had made love together so heatedly the previous weekend!—but nevertheless he was a man who kept himself totally self-contained, and he did that by placing a barrier about his emotions.

A barrier that seemed to crumble, and be about to fall, the more time the two of them spent together.

A barrier he now seemed to be willing to

drop completely in order to share something from his past with her.

A barrier that she now realised had come into existence because of that past?

How could Andy *not* listen if it gave her an insight into why Darius was the way that he was?

She settled back on the sofa, waiting patiently as she watched Darius gather his thoughts together before he began speaking.

'I took your advice last Sunday evening and made Xander tell me everything. I now realise…' He paused, shaking his head. 'I should really start at the beginning, not the end.' He sighed. 'My mother and father met at some business conference: he was CEO of his own company; she was PA to one of the other men attending the business conference. The attraction was instant, and the two of them had a brief week-long relationship. Two months later my mother had to go to him and tell him that she was pregnant with Xander and me. My father had forgotten to mention that he was already engaged to marry someone else at the time, the only daughter of a close business associate, so he wasn't exactly overjoyed at the news of Catherine's pregnancy.'

No, Andy could see that might have been a bit awkward.

'My mother refused to have the abortion Lomax instantly offered to pay for,' Darius continued harshly. 'And Lomax refused to marry her. But he did offer, in exchange for her silence, to pay her off. His intention being, I suppose, to carry on with his engagement and marriage. Except pregnancies, especially twins, have a way of showing themselves.' He grimaced. 'The fiancée's father was also a friend of the man my mother worked for and— Well, I'm sure you can guess the rest. The father found out what sort of man Lomax Sterne was, the daughter broke off the engagement, and my father decided to marry my mother after all.'

Andy hadn't realised she had been holding her breath until she had to draw air deeply into her lungs before she could manage to speak. 'Because he had realised he loved her?'

'Because he wanted to make her life and the lives of her two sons a living hell for having screwed up his own life!'

Andy's stomach gave a sickening lurch. 'And did he manage to do that?'

'Oh, yes,' Darius confirmed grimly. 'He really was bad news. By the time my mother realised her mistake she was already married to him and too frightened of him and what he might do to Xander and I to even think of daring to leave him. I look a lot like him, you know,' he added bleakly.

Andy had guessed that Darius must favour his father in looks; after all Catherine was extremely fair, and Xander had his mother's colouring, so Darius had to have got his dark hair and those mesmerising topaz eyes from someone else.

He sighed. 'To cut a long and miserable story short, on the night my father died Xander was once again in hospital. He was being kept in overnight, and my mother was staying with him. He had a broken collarbone and concussion, after supposedly falling off his horse.'

Andy's lips felt numb. 'Xander didn't fall off his horse?'

Darius gave a shake of his head. 'My father had beaten him.' He drew in a ragged breath. 'Maybe if he had laid into me a few times he wouldn't have made my mother's and Xander's lives such hell. And I would gladly have taken some of those beatings in Xander's stead.'

Andy could hear a wealth of guilt behind his words. The same guilt she had heard in his voice the previous Sunday when he had spoken so unguardedly with Xander.

'Instead, I think,' Darius continued heavily, 'because I looked like him, my father thought

I was like him too, and that he could mould me into his own image.'

'He didn't succeed,' Andy assured him forcefully.

'No.' Darius's smile was bleak. 'I may have looked like him, but my nature is much more like my mother's; she has the same ability to shut people out, to present a cold and unemotional front to the world. Whereas Xander looks like my mother, but...'

'I've only met Xander twice, both briefly, but even that was enough to tell me he isn't in the least cruel or physically violent.' Andy frowned; there was no way the easily charming man she had met at the charity dinner was anything like the monster Darius was describing as his father.

'You're right, he isn't.' Darius looked at her approvingly. 'The problem is that he *thinks* he is. Or, perhaps a better way of describing it is that he now *fears* that he might become like him.'

'You can convince him that he won't,' Andy said with certainty.

'Once again, I appreciate your confidence in my abilities,' Darius drawled. 'And I'm doing my best to do that, I assure you.'

Andy looked up at him searchingly. 'There's more, isn't there...?' she guessed softly.

He nodded grimly. 'What I didn't realise, until Xander made that comment last Sunday evening, was that all these years my mother and Xander have believed that I pushed my father down the stairs the night he died, rather than that he fell down them in a drunken stupor. Which is not to say I hadn't thought of it—many times, in fact—for the way he treated my mother and Xander,' he acknowledged bleakly. 'But something always stopped me from following through on the idea.'

'Because you are nothing like your father,' Andy said with certainty. 'Because you simply aren't capable of the violence that he so obviously was.'

Darius drew in a sharp breath, even as he looked down at her searchingly, and saw only sincerity in the clear green of her eyes as she gazed back at him unflinchingly. 'Thank you for that,' he breathed huskily.

'It was never in question,' she assured him firmly. 'We inherit our genes from our parents, yes, but that isn't all that we are. A lot of what we are we make of ourselves. Look at me; no one else in my family was ever interested in ballet, or becoming a dancer of any kind. My sister is an accountant, for goodness' sake!'

'Your sister who doesn't approve of me,' Darius drawled ruefully.

'She doesn't know you,' Andy dismissed. 'Do Xander and your mother know the truth now?' she added softly.

'About my father's death twenty years ago? Yes, I've talked to both of them on the subject this week,' he confirmed as she nodded.

'And has it helped to heal the breach between you and your mother?'

He smiled at Miranda's perception in realising that was the reason for those years of estrangement between them. 'We'll get there, eventually. Unfortunately my mother and I are too much alike—we tend to close ourselves in emotionally. My mother has spent the last twenty years deliberately not asking me for the truth, because she was afraid of hearing it, which in turn caused the emotional disconnection between the two of us.'

'And Xander? Was his accident last weekend really an accident?'

Darius drew his breath in sharply. 'He says it was.'

'And do you believe him?'

'Yes, up to a point I do believe him.' He nodded. 'The truth of the matter is that I've been worried about Xander for a while now, without knowing why. He's been playing even harder than he works, recklessly so, and he works ten-hour days.'

'Like you do.'

'Yes, like I do.' He smiled slightly. 'You know, I thought Xander and I were close, but I had no idea of the torment going on inside his head all these years. This fear that he might one day turn into a monster like our father.' He gave a pained grimace.

'He needs someone to believe in him. Not just you and your mother; that's a given, because you both already love him unconditionally.' She smiled. 'Xander needs someone outside your family, a woman maybe, to love and believe in him.'

Darius eyed her curiously. 'How did you get to be so wise?'

Andy wasn't wise at all; she was talking from personal experience!

Her sister Kim and brother-in-law Colin had been nothing but supportive of her over the past four years, but it was because of Darius, because of his expressed belief in her, that she had found the courage to dare to dance in public again. She would never be as good a dancer as she had once been, and it was going to take the next few weeks of serious training before the gala for her to achieve even an acceptable level for her to appear on a public stage again. But she would never have found the courage to do even that without Darius's belief in her.

A small glimmer of hope had begun to burn inside Andy as Darius talked to her of his parents' marriage, his father's violence, his traumatic childhood, the reason for the emotional breach between himself and his mother all these years and his brother's emotional turmoil now.

A glimmer of hope that Darius, a man she knew never shared his emotions with anyone, *had* to have told her those things, shared those things with her, for a reason...

CHAPTER TEN

'You must be wondering why the hell I'm bothering to burden you with all of this unpleasant family history,' Darius said.

Andy was more than wondering—deep inside, where her hopes and dreams had long been buried, a rainbow of possibilities, which had begun to blossom with her decision to dance again, was now bursting into an array of colours!

'Actually, I was a little concerned initially that you might be going to confess that those rumours about your exotic tastes for whips and paddles in the bedroom were true after all.'

'What?' Darius eyed her incredulously.

She eyed him innocently. 'You mean they aren't true?'

'Of course they aren't tr— You're messing with me, right?' he realised as she grinned at him. 'You do know that it isn't true, but just a load of rubbish printed by the gutter press?'

She nodded, relieved that some of the tension seemed to have left his expression. 'What I was actually wondering—' she held Darius's gaze steadily with hers as she slowly stood up '—is if you're now interested in going back downstairs and bringing your fantasy of making love to me in my dance studio to life.'

'What?' Darius's second gasp was a cross between surprise and laughter.

Miranda's eyes glowed warmly as she slowly crossed the room, hips swaying gently, until she stood just in front of him. 'I did say that it sounds intriguing,' she reminded throatily.

'So you did.' Darius found himself constantly amazed by this woman.

He had just told Miranda all of his awful family history, and instead of being horrified by it, or running as fast as she could in the opposite direction, as she very well might have done, she was instead reminding him of his fantasy with more than a glint of interest in those amazing green eyes.

He closed his own eyes briefly before opening them again. 'Have I told you yet how wonderful I think you are?'

A delicate blush warmed her cheeks as she answered him huskily. 'Not yet, no.'

Darius's arms moved about the slenderness of her waist as he pulled her gently into him.

'Possibly because wonderful doesn't even begin to cover what I think or feel for you. It's because of how I feel about you that I've been able to face the demons of the past. That I'm sure I'll eventually be able to completely heal this breach with my mother. And that's because I—' He broke off, the words proving more difficult to say than he had even imagined they would be.

Except Miranda *deserved* to hear the words. As heartfelt and as often as she would allow him to say them.

He drew in a ragged breath. 'I know we haven't known each other for very long. That it's far too soon for you. That I definitely need to stop being so emotionally closed off, before I can even begin to hope that you'll ever feel the same way about me. That…'

'Darius, will you stop waffling and get to the point?' She groaned her frustration.

He nodded abruptly. 'The *point* is that I've fallen in love with you. Deeply. Completely. For always,' he added with certainty. 'I may be new to this, but what I feel for you is all encompassing. To the point that you now *own* me. And you know what? I don't mind.' He sounded surprised by the admission himself. 'For the first time in my life I actually feel complete. I know exactly what I want and who I want to be with. For the rest of my life. But…'

'Darius?'

'I knew I had to tell you about my family before I said any of this—my father in particular. Because I never want you to think that I've held anything back from you. I want to share all of myself with you, Miranda.'

'Darius…'

'Even the bad bits.'

'Darius, please.'

'Because I do truly love you—more than I ever believed it was possible to love anyone. More than I believed it was possible for *me* to love anyone. And—'

'Darius…!' Andy's exasperation at not being listened to came out as a cross between a protest and a choked laugh. Of happiness. Pure, unadulterated happiness.

Darius loved her.

He genuinely *loved* her!

And she had no doubts that when Darius loved he loved wholeheartedly, with every part of him.

Andy had begun to hope these past few minutes as he talked to her of his family— her heart had more than hoped!—but to hear Darius actually say that he loved her was beyond anything she might ever have imagined.

'I love you too, Darius!' she exclaimed joyfully. 'And if you think your family is a little crazy, then you need to spend some time with my sister and Colin. For starters, they collect antique mirrors, they have a house full of them, and they spend most weekends going to markets and car-boot sales looking for more. My sister is the worst cook in the world. And Colin—'

'You love me?' Darius looked down at her with glowing, hesitant eyes.

It was a hesitancy, an uncertainty that Andy couldn't bear to see in this innately strong and wonderful man whom she loved with every fibre of her being.

'I love you so much, Darius. So, so much,' she repeated huskily even as she placed her hands on his shoulders before moving up onto tiptoe to kiss him.

It started as a slow and wondrous kiss, but quickly developed into so much more as the passion instantly flared between the two of them, and they lost themselves in the pleasure of each other's arms and love.

'Marry me, Miranda,' Darius murmured a long time later as the two of them lay in each other's arms on the sofa together.

Andy looked up at him with wide eyes. 'You want to marry me?'

He gave a happy laugh. 'Where did you *think* this conversation was going, Miranda?' He pretended some of his old sternness.

'I— Well, I—'

'I trust you didn't think I was going to let you take me down to your studio and ravish my body, and then just let you walk away when you'd used me all up?'

'Ah.' Andy felt the warmth of a blush enter her cheeks. 'Regarding that ravishment…'

Darius saw the uncertainty in the green eyes that couldn't quite meet his gaze, along with that telling blush to her cheeks. 'Miranda, are you—? Is it possible that you're—?'

'Still a virgin? Yes.' She buried her embarrassed face against his chest. 'I was going to tell you, of course.'

'Well, I should hope so!'

'It's just not the sort of thing you blurt out to a man who you think just wants—well, who just wants…'

'I get the picture, Miranda,' he drawled ruefully, totally thrown—enchanted—by the thought of his virgin bride. Except she hadn't said yes to his marriage proposal yet…

Darius sat up to move down onto his knees on the carpet beside the sofa before taking both of her hands in his.

'Will you do me the honour of becoming

my wife, Miranda?' he prompted seriously. 'Will you marry me, and be with me, live with me for the rest of our lives, be the mother of our children?'

It was more, so much more, than Andy had ever dreamed of. That Darius loved her was miracle enough, that he wanted her to be his wife, to be with and live with him always, to have his children, was happiness beyond measure.

'Oh, yes, Darius, of course I'll marry you.' Her eyes were blurred with tears of happiness as she launched herself into his arms, overbalancing him so that they both fell onto the carpet, followed by complete silence apart from their happy sighs and the wondrous murmurings of their love for each other.

EPILOGUE

'IT'S ALL GOING to be fine, Darius.' Kim reached out to firmly grasp his hands in hers as he peered tensely from the theatre box down onto the stage as they waited for Miranda to make her appearance as Odette. 'I haven't said this to you before, but your love and belief in Andy are what has made tonight possible,' her sister added huskily. 'And I will be forever grateful to you because of it.'

Darius and Kim had developed a friendship over the past three weeks, mainly because of the deep love they both felt for Miranda. The same deep love that had made Kim distrust him that first night at the restaurant, but which now gave the two of them, and Colin, a deep family bond.

It had been the happiest three weeks of Darius's life, his love, and admiration and pride for Miranda growing stronger every day.

His love because somewhere in amongst

the chaos the two of them had managed to organise a wedding for next month, and in just two weeks' time he would finally claim his virgin bride.

Admiration because Miranda had found the courage to go with him to the police about Tia Bellamy. The other woman had vehemently denied Miranda's accusation at first, but broken down and confessed when informed that several other people had come forward—with a little helpful nudge from Darius, after he had made his own investigation into the other woman's behaviour—with reports of the other woman's vindictiveness, to a degree that the ballet company had now suspended Tia's contract while the investigation continued.

Miranda, as he had known she would, had remained strong throughout that ordeal.

And he was so proud of her for the way in which she had battled to overcome and conquer the years of not dancing, by pushing herself to the limit and beyond with hours and hours of punishing rehearsal in preparation for tonight's performance.

Not just for herself, she had told him, but also for him. Because he had believed in her when she hadn't.

Was it any wonder, knowing that *he* was the reason Miranda had found the courage and will to dance in public again, that he now felt so nervous he thought he might actually be physically ill?

'*Courage, mon brave.*' Xander placed a reassuring hand on Darius's shoulder, nowhere near physically recovered, but having managed to hobble to the box in the theatre with the help of his crutches. 'Andy is going to be amazing,' he added with certainty.

All of Darius's family, and Miranda's, were sitting together in the family box: Xander, Kim and Colin, and his mother and Charles. Because they *were* a family now. All of them. Brought together by the deep love he and Miranda felt for each other.

If anything Darius was even more in love with her now than he had been three weeks ago.

'Here we go,' Xander murmured as the lights dimmed and the curtain began to rise.

Andy's heart was beating wildly in her chest as the curtains lifted in front of where she stood poised in the centre of the stage, the opening bars of the music beginning to play softly, the audience falling expectantly silent.

Andy froze as she looked out at that sea of faces, her heart now pounding loudly, a buzzing in her ears, her stomach churning as she wondered if she was going to be able to do this, after all.

And then she looked up into the box, where she knew Darius was sitting with their families, a calm falling over her as she saw his love for her glowing in his face.

Love and pride.

The same love and pride Darius could see shining for him in Miranda's expression before her shoulders straightened and she began to dance. For him. Only for him. She was a delicate white swan, flying nimble and free across the stage, every movement graceful and perfect.

His Miranda…

* * * * *

LARGER-PRINT BOOKS!

GET 2 FREE LARGER-PRINT NOVELS PLUS
2 FREE GIFTS!

❧ HARLEQUIN®

Romance

From the Heart, For the Heart

YES! Please send me 2 FREE LARGER-PRINT Harlequin® Romance novels and my 2 FREE gifts (gifts are worth about $10). After receiving them, if I don't wish to receive any more books, I can return the shipping statement marked "cancel." If I don't cancel, I will receive 4 brand-new novels every month and be billed just $4.84 per book in the U.S. or $5.24 per book in Canada. That's a savings of at least 19% off the cover price! It's quite a bargain! Shipping and handling is just 50¢ per book in the U.S. and 75¢ per book in Canada.* I understand that accepting the 2 free books and gifts places me under no obligation to buy anything. I can always return a shipment and cancel at any time. Even if I never buy another book, the two free books and gifts are mine to keep forever.

119/319 HDN F43Y

Name	(PLEASE PRINT)

Address	Apt. #

City	State/Prov.	Zip/Postal Code

Signature (if under 18, a parent or guardian must sign)

Mail to the **Harlequin® Reader Service:**
IN U.S.A.: P.O. Box 1867, Buffalo, NY 14240-1867
IN CANADA: P.O. Box 609, Fort Erie, Ontario L2A 5X3

Want to try two free books from another line?
Call 1-800-873-8635 or visit www.ReaderService.com.

* Terms and prices subject to change without notice. Prices do not include applicable taxes. Sales tax applicable in N.Y. Canadian residents will be charged applicable taxes. Offer not valid in Quebec. This offer is limited to one order per household. Not valid for current subscribers to Harlequin Romance Larger-Print books. All orders subject to credit approval. Credit or debit balances in a customer's account(s) may be offset by any other outstanding balance owed by or to the customer. Please allow 4 to 6 weeks for delivery. Offer available while quantities last.

Your Privacy—The Harlequin® Reader Service is committed to protecting your privacy. Our Privacy Policy is available online at www.ReaderService.com or upon request from the Harlequin Reader Service.

We make a portion of our mailing list available to reputable third parties that offer products we believe may interest you. If you prefer that we not exchange your name with third parties, or if you wish to clarify or modify your communication preferences, please visit us at www.ReaderService.com/consumerchoice or write to us at Harlequin Reader Service Preference Service, P.O. Box 9062, Buffalo, NY 14269. Include your complete name and address.

HRLP13R

LARGER-PRINT BOOKS!
GET 2 FREE LARGER-PRINT NOVELS PLUS
2 FREE GIFTS!

HARLEQUIN

super romance®

More Story...More Romance

YES! Please send me 2 FREE LARGER-PRINT Harlequin® Superromance® novels and my 2 FREE gifts (gifts are worth about $10). After receiving them, if I don't wish to receive any more books, I can return the shipping statement marked "cancel." If I don't cancel, I will receive 6 brand-new novels every month and be billed just $5.69 per book in the U.S. or $5.99 per book in Canada. That's a savings of at least 16% off the cover price! It's quite a bargain! Shipping and handling is just 50¢ per book in the U.S. or 75¢ per book in Canada.* I understand that accepting the 2 free books and gifts places me under no obligation to buy anything. I can always return a shipment and cancel at any time. Even if I never buy another book, the two free books and gifts are mine to keep forever.

139/339 HDN F46Y

Name	(PLEASE PRINT)

Address		Apt. #

City	State/Prov.	Zip/Postal Code

Signature (if under 18, a parent or guardian must sign)

Mail to the **Harlequin® Reader Service:**
IN U.S.A.: P.O. Box 1867, Buffalo, NY 14240-1867
IN CANADA: P.O. Box 609, Fort Erie, Ontario L2A 5X3
Are you a current subscriber to Harlequin Superromance books and want to receive the larger-print edition?
Call 1-800-873-8635 today or visit www.ReaderService.com.

* Terms and prices subject to change without notice. Prices do not include applicable taxes. Sales tax applicable in N.Y. Canadian residents will be charged applicable taxes. Offer not valid in Quebec. This offer is limited to one order per household. Not valid for current subscribers to Harlequin Superromance Larger-Print books. All orders subject to credit approval. Credit or debit balances in a customer's account(s) may be offset by any other outstanding balance owed by or to the customer. Please allow 4 to 6 weeks for delivery. Offer available while quantities last.

Your Privacy—The Harlequin® Reader Service is committed to protecting your privacy. Our Privacy Policy is available online at www.ReaderService.com or upon request from the Harlequin Reader Service.

We make a portion of our mailing list available to reputable third parties that offer products we believe may interest you. If you prefer that we not exchange your name with third parties, or if you wish to clarify or modify your communication preferences, please visit us at www.ReaderService.com/consumerschoice or write to us at Harlequin Reader Service Preference Service, P.O. Box 9062, Buffalo, NY 14269. Include your complete name and address.

HSRLP13R